Praise for
Mike Blakely

"Blakely's style grabs the reader from the first page. His characters are interesting, real, and believable. Since I've been around I've seen the 'Western' declared dead three times. Young writers like Blakely will keep it alive and expanding."
         —Don Coldsmith on *Too Long at the Dance*

"I was enthralled...full bodied and heartbreakingly real."
         —Thomas Fleming, author of *Wages of Fame*

"A fresh and wonderful new voice."
         —Norman Zollinger,
           Spur Award–winning author of
           Chapultepec and *Not of War Only*

Forge Books by Mike Blakely

THE
SNOWY RANGE GANG

Mike Blakely

FORGE®

A TOM DOHERTY ASSOCIATES BOOK
NEW YORK

This is a work of fiction. All the characters and events portrayed in this book are fictitious, and any resemblance to real people or events is purely coincidental.

THE SNOWY RANGE GANG

Copyright © 1991, 1996 by Mike Blakely

Cover art by Dave Henderson

A Forge Book
Published by Tom Doherty Associates, LLC
175 Fifth Avenue
New York, NY 10010

www.tor-forge.com

Forge® is a registered trademark of Tom Doherty Associates, LLC.

ISBN: 978-0-7653-8855-1

First Forge Edition: May 1996

Printed in the United States of America

P1

One

Nine parts pistol and one part scattergun. Claude Duval judged his Le Mat grapeshot revolver the showpiece of his collection. He sat on the porch and tinkered with it as rain washed the pine-studded hills of his ranch and cooled the Laramie Plains below.

His finger drew the trigger in, his thumb holding the hammer back, easing it down on the firing pin. The action sounded like a clicking symphony of machined parts to Claude's ears, accompanied by the patter of raindrops on the shakes. His nostrils flared and took in the clean aroma of rain come down from the thunderclouds, pierced by the bite of gun oil.

Reaching under the bench, he touched the whiskey bottle but passed it over for the oil can. In his younger years he might have been well lit by this hour on a lazy day like today. But, at thirty-six, Claude Duval was finally learning to temper his bad habits. His fingers took in the oil can and let the whiskey bottle lie.

He put the hummingbird spout of the can to the revolving cylinder of the Le Mat and clicked the bottom of the can once, applying a single drop with restrained precision. To spread the oil, he turned the cylinder—an odd oversize design that chambered nine .42-caliber pistol rounds. The Le Mat didn't pack the knockdown power of a Smith & Wesson Russian or a Colt Peacemaker, but it chambered nine rounds instead of six. Three extra shots could come in handy these days, Claude thought, with every gun-lugging rustler on the range thinking six-shooters.

And the Le Mat still had a wild card to play. Instead of a solid steel pin, its cylinder revolved around a short, smoothbore, twenty-gauge shotgun barrel loaded with a blast of double aught. It was twice-barreled, over and under, the pistol barrel on top, the shot barrel underneath. The weapon was like a six-shooter and a half, with a sawed-off shotgun thrown in for grins.

Claude knew why the grapeshot revolver had never caught on. It had a movable tang on the hammer that the shooter flipped one way to fire the pistol rounds and the other way to fire the shotgun barrel. Under rough use, the tang had a tendency to break off, and then the hammer wouldn't fire anything. Still, it was the kind of piece Claude liked—one with unusual features.

He owned a Cooper's ring-trigger pepperbox, a six-shooter with six barrels; a Sharps carbine with a coffee mill built into the stock; a Jarre pinfire harmonica gun with a sliding magazine that looked like a mouth harp ... They weren't worth much, but he didn't collect them for their pecuniary value. He just liked guns. He kept them in mint condition, the finest pieces hidden under the floorboards of his new frame house.

The Le Mat grapeshot revolver was his favorite. He loved to feel it work in his hand, yet every time he did, he wanted to kick himself for not thinking of the idea on his own. A shotgun barrel in the middle of the cylinder. Genius.

Claude had dreamed for years of inventing some firearm that would carry his name into posterity, but the only idea he had ever come up with was a thing he called the Duval Derringer—a pocket pistol that could be made to shoot backward as well as forward.

The idea had come to him a few years ago down in Texas when a cow thief he had been tracking snuck up on him in camp, disarmed him, and shot him with his own Colt. He remembered thinking just before the slug hit him in the chest that if his pistol could have been rigged to shoot backward at the flip of a lever or something, the rustler would have shot himself right in the eye. As it happened, though, he was lung-shot with his own gun and left for dead. Luckily, a couple of cowboys hunting strays had heard the shot and came to investigate. They took him to Mobeetie, where an army doctor from Fort Elliott announced he would probably die overnight. When Claude came around, he found a pine box at his bedside. They were efficient at burials in Mobeetie, but Claude had disappointed them.

Of course, the Duval Derringer would never reach production. Too dangerous. Some innocent fool would flip the switch the wrong way and shoot himself, sure as the world. Claude would have to think of something better.

He put the oil can down and pulled his watch from his vest pocket. Three minutes past the half hour. Time for a swallow. He picked up the whiskey bottle, pulled the stopper, and smelled the aroma as he put the spout to his lips. He doled the liquor out as he would oil on a fine collectible. Too much lubrication could break down a good grip, ruin one's stock.

Claude was forever thinking guns, hoping an idea for a new weapon would strike him one day. A patent in his name would sure show the folks back home.

Every man in the Duval family of Texas—except Claude—claimed a title of some kind. His father was Judge Duval, his brothers Senator and Major Duval. The only word he had ever heard spoken before his name was "Sabinal." And that wasn't a title, just a nickname given to him by his old friend Dusty Sanderson. He and Dusty had once owned a small ranch on the Sabinal River, west of San Antonio. Pretty place. Part of the Lost Maples woods grew on the ranch and turned beautiful colors in the fall. But they had lost that place to creditors.

A few years after that, he lost Dusty, too, and his life took some turns he had never planned.

Claude may not have cared where he stood with the Duval family—Dusty had never cared—but he was thankful to have his clan's good looks. He measured over six feet with his boots on, filled out the shoulders of his riding jacket, and looked at the world through twinkling sky-blue eyes. Those eyes were sprouting a lot of crow's-feet these days, but he had squinted at a lot of horizons. His eagle's nose was a Duval trademark, and his jaw was perhaps the finest in the family.

He knew his kin disapproved of him and the life he had chosen, so he had cultivated his own appearance, as if to set himself apart from the other Duval men. They were fond of ostentatious whiskers, so Claude had made a ritual of shaving. His brothers cropped their hair short, so he grew his in waving locks that fell on his shoulders.

He didn't even pronounce the family name the way his kin did. With the judge and the senator and the major, it was *dyu-VALLE*. With Sabinal Claude, it was just plain old *DOO-val*.

"You know, Sabinal," Dusty had told him one hot day on the trail to Dodge, both of them riding drag in the wake of the herd, "you could have stayed home and sat in the shade of your family tree. But look at you now, ridin' out in the sunshine."

"Yeah," Claude had replied, "if only I could see it through all this damned alkali dust."

When they were fifteen, Claude and Dusty had quit school in Austin, left their homes, and hired on with a South Texas ranch. After the war, when the big trail drives began, they had both made top hands, driving beeves as far north as Montana. It was on a return trip from Montana that they had first stumbled upon these pine-studded hills between the Laramie Plains and the Medicine Bow Mountains.

"If I could make a ranch go," Dusty had said, "this is where I'd put it. A man could tolerate poverty in a pretty place like this."

That had been more than a dozen years ago. It had taken him that long to make up his mind to leave Texas. Too many Dyu-VALLES down there looking down their Roman noses at him. Texas had never been the same, anyway, after Dusty's murder.

Of course, the deciding factor had nothing to do with his partner's death or his family. He had simply gotten nervous about some back-shooter slipping up on him. He had crossed a lot of hard cases over the years in Texas.

Claude had never intended to go into the stock detective business. It had happened by accident. The first winter after Dusty died, a gang of rustlers stole a herd out from under his nose near a line camp he was in charge of on a Panhandle ranch. Claude had taken out after them without even going for help, figuring the outlaw Giff Dearborn was ramrodding the rustlers. Dearborn was part of the reason Dusty had been murdered, and Claude wanted his scalp.

He trailed the rustlers until he caught them drunk in camp in New Mexico. They had already lost most of the cattle to stampede. It wasn't Giff Dearborn's bunch, but Claude brought them back to Texas, anyway, spending two sleepless days in the saddle guarding them. Most of the stolen cattle drifted back to home range. The affair made him look real good and started a lot of talk.

The next time a bunch of cattle turned up missing, the boss came looking for Claude Duval. "Sabinal," he said, "rustlers damn near cleaned out that herd down on the South Branch. I want you to go after 'em."

"Hell, boss, call the Texas Rangers. I ain't no regulator."

"You're a Duval, aren't you?"

"Damned if I ain't. What's that got to do with anything?"

"We need your kind of Duval backbone. Some of the other outfits have agreed to throw in for your wages. A hundred dollars for every cow thief you can kill or put in jail."

He could no more pass up earnings like those than he could let his family name get the better of him. His brothers had been Confederate heroes, his father a decorated volunteer in the war with Mexico. Claude's would be a range war.

He had only killed a couple of rustlers over the years, and then only to save his own skin. But he had sent dozens to jail. Maybe that was his mistake. Men tended to get out of prison sooner or later and drift back to their old ranges. Things had gotten hot for Claude down in Texas. It was well that he had come north.

He was starting something new in Wyoming. No more chasing rustlers. He had bought the section Dusty had been particularly fond of, here in the foothills of the Medicine Bows. He planned to run a few cattle and train some horses through the summer, maybe do a little gunsmithing.

When fall came, he would guide hunters into the Medicine Bows. A lot of those rich easterners were looking for sport out West nowadays. This was the perfect place to give them their taste of it. Laramie was only twenty miles to the northeast. He could pick them up at the Union Pacific depot and bunk them here before starting into the mountains. The Medicine Bows teemed with game: elk, deer, bear, lion, even mountain sheep.

He had a lot to do before the best fall hunting began. He had barns and corrals to build, horses and pack mules to buy. He needed to get up into the mountains to scout for the best hunting. But today he was content to sit on the porch and tinker with his guns. He wasn't going to stand out in the rain and dig post holes.

Looking down the irons of the Le Mat, Claude swept the Laramie Plains until a moving figure caught his eye. A yellow slicker emerged from the mist about half a mile away, the rider coming at a lope up the road.

"Now, who the hell is that?" he said to himself. He rose, shoved the Le Mat under his belt, and went into the house to choose a couple of weapons. He picked a Model 76 Winchester and a double-barreled shotgun. It didn't hurt to be careful. He didn't know anybody around here yet.

When he stepped back out onto the porch, the rider was within rifle range and still coming in plain view. The man obviously wasn't looking for trouble. Probably a social call. Some friendly neighbor wanting to sip a little whiskey on a rainy day.

But as the yellow slicker neared, Claude began to see recognizable features. By the time the visitor pulled rein in front of the house, he knew who it was.

Two

❧

"You've strayed off your range, Bob."
Bob Steck dropped from the saddle, stomped up
the porch steps, and shook Claude's hand. He
took his hat off to slap the rain from it, revealing
his thinning crop of gray hair. "I saw your ad-
vertisement for hunters in the Laramie paper. I
was hopin' it would be the same Claude Duval
I knew in Texas. The world ain't got room for
another." His darting eyes caught the whiskey
bottle, and he smiled.

Claude had worked for Bob Steck a few times
as a stock detective, recovering dozens of stolen
cattle and breaking up a ring of cow thieves.
Steck owned one of the biggest ranches on the
Texas coast. He was about fifty-five years old,
but wild as a young buck, and used to doing
whatever he damn well pleased. He was rather
small, but built solid. He stayed in better condi-

tion than most twenty-year-olds, though he didn't work at it. He seemed to build muscle just going about his business, and every move he made was a thing of sure grace.

"So you came to hunt, did you?" Claude asked, picking up the bottle.

Steck grinned. "Yes. I sure did."

"Last I heard you were in Europe."

The rancher threw his wet slicker aside and took the whiskey bottle from Claude. "I had some trouble with some neighbors. Shot one of them in town one night, and I figured I needed a vacation about then."

"Have things cooled off?"

Steck nodded. "I made restitution, and the fellow I shot dropped the charges against me. Hell, we even went partners in a new venture. Raisin' bremmer crossbreeds." He put the neck of the bottle in his mouth and turned it upside down.

"What kind of crossbreeds?"

"Bremmers." Steck picked up the double barrel as he sat on the bench.

"Brimmers?"

"No, bremmers."

"Spell it."

"B-R-A-H-M-A-S."

Claude squinted one eye. "That spells brahmas, don't it?"

"Well, 'bremmers' is easier on my conversation. Didn't you ever see that bremmer bull I had at the ranch?"

"I don't recall. What did he look like?"

"If you'd have seen him, you'd remember. Big gray bull with floppin' ears, enough dewlap and sheath to carpet your parlor, and a big hump on his shoulder."

"You mean like a buffalo?"

"No, more like a camel. But not the kind the army imported before the war. More like those two-hump camels."

Claude's eyebrows rose. "These bremmers have got two humps?"

"No, just one, but it sort of flops over to one side like a hump on one of them two-hump camels."

"I never saw anything like that," Claude said, lifting his flat-brimmed hat to rake his long hair back. "Where'd you get 'em?"

"They come from India. I bought that first one I had from a fellow in South Carolina after the war. I got to studying that bull, and I liked what I saw. You know how a longhorn will sweat around the nose?"

"Yeah."

"Well, this bremmer would sweat all over. And he'd sweat poison to ticks. When he'd sweat, they'd just drop off of him like rain."

Claude adjusted the Le Mat under his belt. "I guess that's good."

"Good, hell! That's a revolution in Texas beef! Most people haven't figured it out yet, Sabinal, but ticks is what causes Texas fever. I'm sure of it. Now, if we can breed that poisonous sweat into some bremmer-longhorn crosses, we can wipe out Texas fever and open the market for Texas cattle again."

Claude smiled and sank to the bench. Steck always had some revolution in mind. "Where you gonna get your breed stock?"

"Already got 'em. Had 'em, anyway. When I was on the lam in Europe, I figured I might just as well make use of the trip and take a tramp steamer over to India to see if I might buy some bremmer bulls. That's the damnedest, dirtiest country in the world, Sabinal. Don't ever go there."

"Worse than Mexico?"

"Oh, hell, you'd think Laredo was paradise next to Bombay. But the thing is, they've got bremmers runnin' loose in the streets. Fool Hindus won't eat 'em. Say they're sacred. They tame those bremmers like pet dogs, always hand-feedin' 'em and huggin' on 'em and what-not, but they won't eat 'em. Wouldn't even sell me any if I said I was gonna breed beef cattle with 'em. I had to lie and tell 'em I wanted those sacred bremmers to spread their Hindu religion around Texas, although whatever the hell their religion's all about, I don't know, and don't want to know. If it's against eatin' beef, I'm against it."

Claude smiled. "How many of these bremmers did you get?"

"Fifty bulls and a dozen heifers. By the time I sailed 'em across the Atlantic, I had almost a thousand dollars invested in every head. Then the damned Department of Agriculture says I've got to quarantine 'em and have a bunch of tests run to make sure they ain't diseased. So I quarantined 'em on Matagorda Island, right off the coast from my ranch, and that's when all hell broke loose."

"They get sick?"

"No, they got rustled! I had one of my hired boys out there to watch 'em for a couple of weeks. Well, when I sailed over to the island with this government inspector who was gonna run disease tests on 'em, I found my hired man shot dead and all my bremmers gone."

Claude squirmed a little on the hard bench. "How did they get 'em off the island?"

"Stolt a ferry boat and floated 'em across the bay to my ranch. We found the ferry owner shot dead, too. Whoever stolt 'em loaded 'em on a northbound. That's what brought me here."

Claude's eyebrows drew together. He didn't like the turn this conversation had taken. "I thought you said you came here to hunt."

"I did. Hunt rustlers. I traced those stolen bremmers up the railroads all the way to Laramie. Wasn't hard. They tend to draw attention. The rustlers put 'em off at Laramie and herded 'em west. I was about to take out after 'em alone when I saw your name in the newspaper. Imagine that. The best regulator in Texas shows up right in my trail way the hell up in Wyoming just when I need him!"

Claude stood and yanked his shotgun away from the rancher. "I'm not for hire," he said sternly. "I came up here to get out of that business." He picked up the Winchester and returned both weapons to the gun rack inside the door.

"You haven't even let me make an offer," Steck said. "I'll pay a hundred a head for every bremmer recovered and two hundred a head for every rustler. You don't have to go it alone, either. I'll come with you."

"No, you won't, because I ain't goin'," Claude insisted. He pulled his watch from his pocket. It wasn't time for a swallow yet, but he snatched the bottle up, anyway. His past hadn't taken long in catching up.

"All right, two hundred for every bremmer and five hundred for every rustler. You stand to make thousands, Sabinal."

"I stand to get killed. You've already got two dead men on your hands. I don't want to be the next."

They sat and argued, sipped whiskey, and watched the rain until Claude convinced Bob Steck that he would never chase another rustler. He invited Steck to stay overnight, but the rancher insisted on getting back to Laramie to find a real stock detective. Grousing, the old Texan put his slicker back on, tightened his saddle cinch, and mounted. But just as he was getting ready to use his spurs, he reached into his saddle pocket.

"Say, Sabinal, you know a thing or two about guns. What can you tell me about this?" He pulled something from the saddle pouch. "Of course, now, don't let me put you out none . . ."

Claude caught the empty brass shell casing that Steck tossed to him under the porch roof. It was a big one, about the size of a man's finger. He recognized the caliber and the distinctive necked outline, felt a long-buried pang of hatred come back to life. "A .44-90. Made for the old Model 73 Sharps Creedmoor." His glare rose to pierce Steck's eyes. "Where'd you get this?"

"Matagorda Island. We figured it was the shell used to kill my man I had guardin' the bremmers."

"What made you figure that?"

"We found it in his hand. We figured the killer put it there. That dead ferry operator had one in his hand, too."

Claude's jaws seized up on him for a second,

and his fist clenched tight around the brass shell. He felt the heat of Texas on his face again. He spit into the rain and forgot all about hunting deer and elk.

"Bob," he said, "you just hired yourself a regulator."

Three

∽o∾

Claude pushed his empty plate away and sloshed a shot of whiskey into his coffee cup. "We don't do anything until we get an answer to that telegram," he said to Steck.

The rancher frowned and sighed. "Who is this fellow Wolverton, anyway?"

It was midnight, and they had arrived in Laramie wet and hungry. One good thing about working for Bob Steck, Claude thought. The rancher didn't skimp on grub. The food at the Depot Cafe was the best in town.

"They used to call him Lone Wolf," Claude muttered. "He was a stock detective and a bounty hunter years ago, before I got into the business."

"You callin' him in to help?"

Anger glinted in Claude's eyes. "Hell, no. I didn't send the telegram *to* Wolverton. I sent it *about* him. He's supposed to be servin' a life sentence in the Texas state pen. But that Creedmoor cartridge you found in the hands of those dead men—that was his sign."

"Sign?"

Claude nodded, his eyes staring into his coffee cup. "When he was regulatin' for those big outfits years ago, Wolverton would take his rustlers out at long range with a 73 model Sharps Creedmoor. He'd Lone-Wolf 'em—that's what they called it. After he killed 'em he'd just leave 'em lay and put that cartridge in their hand as a warning to other rustlers. Sharps only made that caliber rifle for a few years and they're hard to come by. When you found a Sharps .44-90 shell in some poor dead bastard's hand, there was no mistakin' who'd done it. It was known as Wolverton's sign from West Texas to Montana."

"How come I never heard of this Lone Wolf?" Steck said.

"He never worked down your way before. Besides, he didn't go in much for publicity. Laid low most of the time."

"You think he stolt my bremmers?"

"I sent that telegram to the prison to find out whether or not he's still there. If he's out, I'd say he's the man you're after."

Steck poured his coffee from his cup to his saucer and blew across it to cool it. "You know him?"

"Never actually met the son of a bitch. Seen him, though."

"What's he look like?"

"Big man. Carries a lot of weight. Got about a quarter Indian blood. Pawnee, I believe."

Steck sensed Duval holding something back.

The range detective had ridden all the way to Laramie in a brood, refusing to say much until now. "What landed him in prison?"

Claude looked at the wall over the rancher's head. "His style of regulatin'. Never asked any questions, just shot his men dead from four, five hundred yards out. He was a back-shooter. Took 'em square between the shoulders every time. That .44-90 shoots a four-hundred-fifty-grain bullet. It'll tear a man wide open. Down in the Panhandle, dozen years ago, he mistook a cowboy for a rustler he was after. Killed him and left that cartridge in his hand. They should have hung him, but he turned himself in and gave a guilty plea, so the judge went easy on him and sentenced him to life."

Steck grunted. "So now he's escaped and gone from regulatin' to rustlin'."

"Looks that way."

"He must have lost his touch in prison. Those two we found dead weren't shot too clean."

The detective's sky-blue eyes narrowed and settled on the rancher's face. "That don't sound like Lone Wolf. He was steady."

"Maybe it ain't him at all. Maybe it's some imitator."

"We'll know when we get that telegram."

The Western Union boy found Claude bearded with shaving soap the next morning in his hotel room. The regulator tipped the boy, read the telegram alone in his room. He stared at the wall for a while, the page in his hand. He took an eye-opening swig from his flask, finished shaving, then went next door to rouse Steck from bed.

"Looks like Wolverton's our man," Claude said.

Steck's silver hair was standing on end. He had taken quite a few drinks at the Chugwater Saloon last night. He held the telegram at arm's length and squinted at it.

"Oh, hell," Claude said, snatching the page from the rancher, "when are you gonna get yourself some readin' glasses?" He read the telegram aloud:

"Lone Wolf model prisoner. Started Sunday school. Read entire prison library. Captain debating team. Full pardon by governor six weeks ago."

"That's about the time I got back with the bremmers," Steck said.

Claude shook his head and hissed. "They're pardonin' murderers now, Bob. Time was they'd hang 'em."

The rancher rubbed his face. "I'll still hang 'em, by God." When his eyes finally focused, he was surprised to see Claude smiling, but with more deviltry than joy. "Did you cut yourself shavin'?"

"Huh?" Claude stroked his face and felt blood smear under his fingers. "I guess so. Hurry up and get dressed. Let's go get those bremmers back."

While Steck bought saddle horses, pack mules, and supplies, Claude visited the shop of his only friend in Laramie, a gunsmith he had swapped collectibles with. The brass bell on the door announced his arrival. "Mornin', Phil," he said, raking his long hair back and fixing it in place with his hat.

"Claude!" the fat little gunsmith said. "What brings you to town?"

Claude smiled and shrugged. "Gets lonesome out there in the hills."

Phil put his fat oil-stained hand in Claude's. "With all those guns to keep you company?"

The Texan let out a genuine chuckle. Phil just had a way about him. "To tell you the truth, I thought I'd take one of my old long-range rifles up in the mountains after some elk. You got any Sharps .44-90s?"

The little man's eyes grew round and sparkled. "You're the second man to ask in two weeks! What's all the interest in these Creedmoors around here all of a sudden? I didn't even know you had one."

"What would I do with the ammunition if I didn't have one? Have you got the shells or not?"

"I found two boxes way in the back, but I sold them to that other fellow."

Claude gritted his teeth and shook his head. "I had my heart set on shootin' the old Creedmoor. Who was this other fellow? Maybe I can get a few rounds from him."

"Stranger," Phil said, shrugging.

"What did he look like?"

"Rough-lookin' little character. Between you and me in height, I guess. Dirty clothes. Bad complexion. You know, pockmarks. Haven't seen him since. I don't think you'll find him around here."

"Where was he goin'?"

"He didn't say, and I didn't ask. Say, what's that under your belt?"

Claude proudly drew the Le Mat and handed

it to the gunsmith. He had found it under his belt the day before when he mounted to leave his ranch with Bob Steck. Instead of leaving it in the house, he had decided to bring it with him. It would make a nice addition to the Marlin repeater and the matched pair of .44-caliber Smith & Wesson Russians he had packed for the trip.

"You didn't tell me you had a Le Mat!" Phil said. "Say, this is a nice piece! You're a real collector, Claude, if you've got one of these *and* a .44 Sharps Creedmoor."

When he left the gun shop, Claude put the grapeshot revolver in his saddlebag and mounted the big paint stallion he called Casino. The horse had caught his eye the day he arrived in Laramie. He had always admired paint horses but had never owned one because Dusty didn't like them. He remembered well the highest praise Dusty had ever given to a paint horse: "His hide might make a good rug." But Dusty had been dead eleven years now and Claude figured he could ride whatever kind of horseflesh he wanted.

A day hadn't gone by that he hadn't thought of his old partner. Things Dusty had said came to him at odd hours, day and night. He remembered the way Dusty rode, walked, laughed. The only thing he couldn't remember was what he looked like. Oh, he could describe him to anybody, to a T. But he couldn't picture him anymore. Hadn't actually seen Dusty Sanderson's face since the day of his murder. He had never mentioned it to anybody, but he felt awful guilty about it. He should have been able to conjure a picture of the man's face at will, but try as he did, it would not come.

He reined Casino up the street and rode to the rail yard stock pens to meet Steck. Yesterday's rain clouds had broken apart and now looked like clean white sheep grazing a blue field. He found Steck sitting on a stockyard fence rail, taking in the sun, talking to one of the hands.

"This is the feller, Sabinal," Steck said, jumping down from the fence.

The stock pen foreman nodded at Claude through the rails. "What can I do for you?"

"I hear you saw some strange cattle here a while back."

"I sure did."

"Mind tellin' me about 'em?"

"I already told him yesterday," the foreman said, pointing at Steck. "Not much to tell, anyway. They looked like a cross between a camel and a big gray mule. About fifty or sixty head, I don't remember the exact count. Three cowboys took 'em off in the middle of the night."

"What about the men? What did they look like?"

The foreman scratched his head. "Didn't get a good look at 'em. It was dark, and I was sort of starin' at those flop-eared cattle."

"Did you see a big feller? Part Indian? Carried a long rifle?"

"Like I say, them cattle sort of got my attention away from everything else." The foreman rolled the quid in his cheek and spit.

"How about a dirty little cowboy with a pock-marked face?"

"That sounds more like the fellers I saw, but like I say, I didn't see any faces up close."

"And they headed west?"

He pointed across the plains. "Seemed to be

headin' toward Big Hollow. Those cattle sure trailed easy. Like a bunch of old pet horses."

They started west across the Laramie Plains, leading their pack train and spare horses. The mules carried grub to last a month and enough ammunition for an extended campaign. Bob Steck had no aversion to spending money for the right cause. He had made and lost half a dozen fortunes in his life.

"You reckon Lone Wolf has put a gang together?" the rancher asked as they trotted across the plains. The wet ground was already pushing up tiny spikes of bright green grass.

"Seems likely, don't it?" Claude said. The gloom from the previous day had lifted from him, and he felt glad to be riding.

"How long you had that horse?" Steck said, admiring Casino.

"Since I come up here."

"You like him?"

"So far. He's got good bottom for a big horse. Mustang blood."

Steck let out a hoot that died somewhere on the prairie. "That ain't no mustang! Mustangs are little!"

"In Texas maybe. But up here they've bred with draft horses the Indians used to run off of the farms in Nebraska. Casino was caught wild on Powder River when he was a colt."

"Somebody sold you a bill of goods, Sabinal. I know a mustang when I see one, and that horse would make two of 'em."

Claude realized, traveling in Steck's good company, that he missed some things about regulating. Riding, camping, reading the sign. Now he was back in it, and his spirits were lifting, but this case still had him worried.

No one other than Lone Wolf Wolverton could have brought Claude out of his retirement as a stock detective. Yet he had to wonder what he had gotten himself into. Some of the evidence pointed to Lone Wolf, but not all of it. He had the Creedmoor shells and the pardon from prison. But there was also the sloppy shooting Steck had told him of and the fact that no one in Laramie could say they had seen Wolverton—only this little fellow with the pockmarked face.

He tried to tell himself it didn't matter. One way or another, this business with the sacred brahma cattle was going to bring him face-to-face with the man called Lone Wolf. Lying on his belly with his Creedmoor in his hands, the old murderer had killed many a man. Claude had waited years to show him how to do it standing up.

Four

~⌒~

The evening shadows fell across Big Hollow, a huge wind-scoured gouge in the Laramie Plains. It ran nine miles east to west, widened to three, and plunged a hundred and fifty feet below the surface of the surrounding plains. It held a little water in its bottom, but it wasn't a rain-carved feature. It was what Claude called a blowout—a wind-hollowed pit—the largest he had ever seen.

He and Bob Steck called on a small ranch near the hollow, hoping for an invitation to stay the night. The rancher, a man old enough to be Bob Steck's daddy, seemed pleased to have their company.

"Put your horses in the barn and bring your bedrolls in the house," he said. "I'll cook some steaks and potatoes for you."

A wind was whipping over the treeless rim of

the hollow, carrying regular spouts of fine sand into the air, but the house was comfortable in spite of the dust, and the old man knew hospitality, breaking out the best whiskey for his guests.

He introduced himself as Jimmy McWhorter and talked nonstop as he cooked supper for three on the rusty wood stove. "Glad you showed up. Had to butcher a heifer last week and ought to eat it before it spoils."

Halfway through the meal, he finally ran out of talk and started asking questions. "Where you boys from?" he asked.

"Texas," Steck answered.

"Goin' huntin'?"

"Huntin' rustlers," Steck replied. "Seen any?"

Claude could only grimace, caught as he was with his mouth full. From now on, he was going to have to make sure Bob didn't do the talking for them. The rancher had never learned when not to advertise.

"Not that I'd know of," McWhorter replied. "What did they look like?"

Claude swallowed a chunk of steak and started carving another bite. "We don't know for sure, but I can tell you what the cattle they stole looked like. Big, gray, humpbacked rascals with dewlaps and flop ears."

McWhorter pounded the table with his fist. "Bremmers?"

The Texans looked at each other. "Well, yes," Steck answered. "How'd you know?"

"Five strangers trailed by here with a herd of 'em. Better than sixty, I'd say, mostly bulls. One heifer was draggin', so they sold her to me cheap. Ten dollars."

"Ten dollars!" Steck shouted.

"Where is she now?" Claude asked. He forced an oversize piece of meat into his mouth.

McWhorter gestured with his fork. "You just bit into a hunk of her."

Steck coughed up a swallow of whiskey and jumped back so quick that his chair slapped against the floor. "You butchered her!" he wheezed.

Claude took to laughing so that he couldn't swallow.

"She took sick and died," McWhorter explained.

The tenderloin in Claude's mouth suddenly lost its flavor, and he swallowed a chunk that felt big as his fist. He grimaced as he pushed his plate away.

"That's a thousand-dollar heifer you butchered!" the rancher said.

Claude picked up Steck's chair. "Now, settle down, Bob, and take your seat. He didn't know that heifer was yours." He turned to McWhorter. "How did you know to call that heifer a bremmer?"

"That's what they called her—them fellers that sold her to me. Said it was some foreign breed that would sweat poison to ticks."

Steck plopped down in his chair, fuming.

"Mr. McWhorter," Claude explained, "those fellers were outlaws. Rustled them bremmers from Bob down in Texas. It would help if you could tell us what they looked like."

McWhorter had a good memory for details. He described all five men, their horses and tack, their chaps, spurs, hats, and guns. There was a pair of redheaded twin brothers, he said, a black man with a cavalry cap, and a squaw wearing a white man's suit.

"The one that done most of the talkin'," he continued, "and I reckon was sort of their leader, was a ugly little cuss looked like his face'd gone through a sausage grinder. Wore shotgun leggin's, gray felt hat all caved in, spurs didn't match. Had a buffalo gun so long he had to cut the end off his saddle boot and I saw the muzzle stickin' out. Had a covered front sight like a railroad tunnel."

"You sure there wasn't a big fellow with 'em?" Claude asked, his eyes glistening with excitement. "Bigger than me, heavyset, part Indian."

The old man shook his head. "No. Just them five. Odd outfit."

When they heard the old man snoring that night, the Texans added up what they knew.

"Whoever rustled those cattle had heard you talk about 'em," Claude said. "Who else would call 'em bremmers and talk about sweatin' tick poison? I figure somebody heard you braggin' about 'em in some saloon down in Texas and decided to go out on Matagorda Island and maverick 'em."

"You still reckon it was Wolverton? McWhorter didn't see anybody that looked like him."

"Wolverton's smart. He could just be layin' low while those five outlaws take all the risk for him. It was three men in Laramie. Now it's four men and a squaw. Wolverton may have put a gang together while he was teachin' Sunday school in prison."

"Maybe Lone Wolf rustled the cattle from

Matagorda Island," Steck suggested, "then sold 'em to the gang that brought 'em up here."

"Maybe. But that little gang leader's carryin' a Creedmoor, and I'm not givin' up yet on it bein' Lone Wolf's gun. I don't know if you believe in hunches, Bob, but I've got one like an itch tellin' me we're gonna meet up with Wolverton before the hand is dealt." He pulled his hat over his eyes.

Steck lay back on his blankets and chuckled. "Damn, that old man can snore. I've heard quieter sawmills."

"Bob," the stock detective said, "I want you to promise me somethin'. When we come up against Wolverton, he's mine."

"Oh, hell, Sabinal. I know what you'll do. You'll march him back to town and let some judge have him."

Claude's hat muffled his voice. "Not this time. Not Wolverton. I intend to press an empty shell into his hand."

They saddled up in front of McWhorter's place at dawn, a hot breakfast in their stomachs.

"They trailed them bremmers west on the north rim of the holler," the old man said. "Looked like they was headin' for the Lafferty Ranch. You'll find it ten miles from here."

They shook the old man's hand and rode toward the mountains along the rim of Big Hollow. An hour into the morning they left the hollow behind and soon saw the barns and bunkhouses of the Lafferty Ranch wavering on the plains in the distance.

A few minutes later, Steck stood in his stirrups at the head of the pack train and leaned over the horn. "Hey!" he shouted, squinting. "Those look like my bremmers!"

Claude trotted up beside him, saw a pasture coming into view over a low roll. Then he spotted the first of the strange-looking cattle. They had horns no bigger than pinecones, ears too big to hold up, and dewlaps hanging like velvet curtains in a whorehouse. He hadn't given Steck's talk about the camel humps much credit until now. They were so big they listed to one side. Each hump looked like a second head growing from the shoulder of each animal. Even the heifers had humps. Some were almost black around the hump and head, others nearly white all over.

"I et one of those for supper last night?" he said.

"I only count forty-five," Steck said. "The rustlers must have sold these and taken the rest somewhere else."

"Don't be too sure," Claude warned. "Better not let on to these folks what we're up to until we ask 'em a few questions. Let me do the talkin'."

They rode through the herd of docile brahmas and found three young cowboys, armed and mounted, waiting to receive them at the main house. As they rode near, an older man stepped out onto the porch. Claude figured him for about forty to forty-five. The working duds he wore showed little wear. His boots held a shine.

The regulator tipped his hat. "Howdy. I'm Claude Duval, your new neighbor down south."

The man nodded, straight-faced. "I'm Ike Lafferty. Been plannin' on payin' you a visit. The boys said they saw a new house down there. What do you run? Cattle or sheep?"

"Just a few cows and horses," Claude said. "I plan to earn most of my wages guidin' hunters in the mountains. This is my first client, Bob Steck."

"What are you huntin' this time of year?" Lafferty asked.

"Bob's after bear," Claude said. He looked over his shoulder. "Those are the damnedest-lookin' cattle back there I ever seen. Where'd you get 'em?"

"Bought 'em from a herd that came through here a while back. The trail boss said he got 'em from an importer in Texas. They're called bremmers. Supposed to be just the thing for the northern ranges."

"They're mine," Steck blurted.

Claude groaned and found the grip of his right-hand Smith & Wesson. "Damn, Bob," he said through his teeth as he eyed the three Lafferty Ranch cowboys and wondered how many others might be watching over their rifle sights from barns or bunkhouses.

"Hell, Sabinal, I don't bluff. Fact is, Mr. Lafferty, you've bought stolen property. Those bremmers are mine. Didn't you ask for a bill of sale?"

"They're not even branded," Lafferty said. "How are you gonna prove those cattle are yours?"

"It's the only blasted herd of bremmers this side of Bombay! I don't have to brand 'em! Besides, I've got bills of sale, shipping records, even a letter from the Department of Agriculture authorizing me to import the son of a bitches." He swung down from his mount, opened the flap of his saddlebag, and removed the papers.

He stalked over to the porch and handed the documents up to Lafferty.

Lafferty shuffled the records, then slapped them against his leg. "Damn! I paid a hundred dollars a head for those bremmers."

"A hundred!" Steck roared. "They're worth ten times that!"

Lafferty paced in front of the house. "That fast-talkin' little bastard took me ... Where's that dog?" he shouted. "I want somethin' to kick!" He charged a pile of stovewood stacked on the front porch, booted chunks among his three cowboys, scattering their broncs. Claude's pack mules bolted and pitched, slinging camp utensils.

Steck jumped onto the porch with Lafferty as the three cowboys started pulling leather. Claude managed to steer Casino clear of the stampede and keep him under control. When he looked back at the porch, he saw Lafferty still fuming and Steck slapping his leg. Bob liked a good laugh as much as a good fight.

"Me and my boys will join you," Lafferty said when the stock had settled down. "Maybe we can get my money back before those rustlers spend it all. They still have sixteen head of your bremmers, too."

"I don't work that way," Claude replied. "A big posse will just give us away. Me and Bob will get your money back for you."

"Well, I'll go with you myself, then," Lafferty said. "Just me."

"I'd rather you left it to us," Claude said.

"Neighbor, I don't care what you'd rather. Those bastards took me. I mean to get 'em. I've lived in this country since it opened up, so don't tell me I can't go after 'em if I want to. Besides, I know the mountains better than you do."

"He's got a point," Steck said. "Wouldn't hurt to have just one other man along."

Claude knew he couldn't keep Lafferty from going, but he wasn't about to let this thing get any further beyond his control. He looked sternly at Lafferty down his eagle's nose. "If you're ridin' with me, you don't flinch without askin' me first."

"Sabinal's the best, Ike," Steck said, already on a first-name basis with the rancher. "We're better off with him leadin' us."

"Fair enough," Lafferty said. "You seem to know what you're doin'. Let's get that pack string back in shape, get somethin' to eat, and get started. I can show you just the way those rustlers went."

Five

❧

The darkened plains sloped up to the mountains, the mountains melding with black clouds, boiling back overhead, engulfing the three men on horseback. To Claude, it felt as if they were riding into a gigantic cave.

Dusty would have taken it as a sign, saying they were riding into a cave of no return, or something like that. Dusty used to look for signs in everything—wind, clouds, animals. Claude had never put much stock in such things, but he liked looking for them, anyway. They reminded him of Dusty and the cowboying days before the stock detective business, before Dusty was murdered for looking too much like the outlaw Giff Dearborn from a distance.

As they rode deeper into the cave of no return, Ike Lafferty described the five outlaws exactly as McWhorter had. "I've heard rumors for years about a gang that summers up around the Snowy Range. Maybe it was them. They've never bothered anybody down here on the Laramie Plains, but rumor has it they rustle a lot of stock as far up as the Wind River country. I guess I should have suspected somethin' funny out of that bunch. That squaw and the colored man with the army cap should have warned me off."

Lafferty knew nothing of anyone matching Lone Wolf's description.

As they climbed the foothills, they began to weave among ponderosa pines, their pace slowing to a walk.

"We'll come to Galloway's Sheep Camp over the next hill," Lafferty said. "I'm not very friendly with Galloway, so watch yourself when we get there."

"Not friendly with your neighbor?" Claude said. "Why not?"

"He runs sheep. Runs too damn many of 'em, if you ask me. Most sheep men are peculiar, but this Galloway is just a mean little cuss. I don't like him. He's Scotch from the old country and stays drunk most of the time. Keeps a little wife with him, and she's mean as him."

When he led the party to the top of the hill, Claude stopped to look over the sheep camp. Ashes shifted where a cabin had stood. The poles of empty corrals lay scattered like splinters. A fire smoldered in a gully near the camp. There were two horses staked to graze, a wagon sheltered under a sheet of canvas. Then he noticed two broken fence rails lashed together to form a cross, planted at the head of a fresh mound of dirt.

"Lordy," Lafferty said, stopping beside the stock detective. "Looks like them outlaws came through here, all right."

"Somebody survived to dig that grave," Claude answered. "How many people lived here?"

"Galloway, his wife, and a hired Indian boy. But the boy usually stayed up in the mountains herdin' sheep."

They eased their pack train down the trail, Claude watching for movement. He passed a broken-down corral fence and noticed signs of blood on the ground. Sheep blood, he surmised. A plain trail led to the smoldering gully. Someone had dragged dead sheep there to burn. The stench of scorched wool was still in the air.

When he got to the grave, he stopped, looking for a name on the cross, finding none. The other riders and the pack train shuffled noisily up behind him. But above the hooves, the squeaking of saddle leather, and the rattle of the packs, he heard the lever of a repeating rifle go through its strokes.

He reached for his side arm as he twisted in the saddle, but the voice stopped him short of drawing the weapon. A smooth, sweet voice, etched with the lilt of Old Scotland. He found its source in a woman who stepped from the gully behind the horsemen, covering them with her rifle, the smoke rising behind her.

"So now you've landed back, have you?" she said, glaring at Ike Lafferty with hard green eyes. She looked small with the big Winchester against her hip, but she seemed sure and agile. Her pretty face was streaked with dirt and sweat. Her grimy green print dress hugged her waist. She wore no hat or bonnet, and tousled brown hair fell over and around her shoulders.

"Now, Correen," Lafferty said, "you don't think I had anything to do with this."

"Who but yourself?" She circled the men to get the best angle on all three, moving like a dancer. "I'm sure I might have thanked you for murderin' my husband, savin' me the trouble, but you never should have killed my dogs and sheep and taken my horses, nor burned my house."

"You've got it wrong, Correen," Lafferty said. "We're on the trail of the gang that did this. Steck here has trailed them all the way from Texas."

"That's right, miss," Steck said.

Claude turned Casino for a better look at the woman. "And just how did you come through this alive?" he asked, his suspicion showing in his face.

The barrel of Correen's Winchester swept quickly around to him, her eyes following. "You're in a more likely way to do the explainin' to me, sir," she said.

Her nerve made Claude smile, and he removed his hand from his pistol butt. He chuckled and raised his hands a little, his reins draped over his left palm. "All right, I see your point. I'll explain . . ."

He told her about the rustled herd of bremmers, the murders in Texas, and the trail to Lafferty Ranch. Thunder rumbled in the mountains and a light rain began to fall.

When she had heard the story, Correen finally lowered her rifle and allowed the men to get their slickers out. "Have you got a tent?" she asked.

Claude nodded.

"Pitch it up over here." She eased the hammer down on the rifle and started toward her wagon.

"You still haven't said how you managed to escape gettin' killed with your husband," Claude said.

She shook her hair over her shoulders. "I wasn't here when it happened." Her eyes narrowed and knifed toward the wooden cross. "My late husband—may God curse his soul— fell from his horse drunk a couple of weeks ago and broke his leg. He couldn't travel, so I took the wagon to town for my messages."

"Your what?"

"My supplies and groceries, you know. Have you never heard the mother tongue?"

"Not the way you speak it. What happened when you came back with your . . . your messages?"

"I found my farm in ashes and my husband dead. I just this mornin' got the last of the sheep dragged together and burned."

Claude reached into his vest pocket. "What do you know about this?" He tossed the Sharps Creedmoor cartridge to Correen.

She snatched the shell from the air, glanced at it briefly. "I've one that matches it. Found in my husband's hand."

"Mrs. Galloway," Bob Steck said, "looks like you and me were visited by the same outlaws."

She tossed the cartridge back to Claude and turned her hardened eyes on Steck. "Don't call me by that devil's name," she said as a large raindrop hit her brow. "You may address me as Correen. I'll take no offense to the familiarity."

When the rain slacked off after dark, Steck and Lafferty left the tent to look after their animals. Claude went out after them, stopping to observe a strange little tent beside the woman's wagon. It looked as though she had taken the bows off her wagon, jammed them in the ground, and covered them with canvas. Through the flapping tent door, he saw her bed inside: straw covered with an old quilt.

He found Correen under the canvas roof that shielded her wagon, washing the supper dishes in a caldron of hot water. "Can I chunk up the fire for you?" he asked, ducking in under the canvas. "Carry some wood or somethin'?"

She glanced at the two revolvers he wore. "Thank you, no. I've gone without a man's help many years now, Mr. Duval."

He had never heard his name spoken with such timbre, but he knew better than to fall for pretty faces and pleasant voices. "Now, don't exaggerate. You're not that old."

"I was taken very young from Scotland. My husband brought me here when I was only fifteen, and I had little to say about it."

His hat was pressing against the canvas, so he took it off, raking his long hair back between his fingers. "Your folks let you marry that young?" He saw Correen pulling at her own tangled trusses, soiled from days of dragging dead sheep. He heard rainwater trickling into a pot under the edge of the canvas and knew she was thinking of making herself presentable.

"I'm sure they did," she said. "We were poor

traveler folk. My father a tinsmith, my mother a basket maker. We never lived in a house. Just wandered about, hawkin' tinware and baskets. My darlin' old mother wanted somethin' better for her children, so she urged me to marry this man, this widower, a sheepherder comin' to America, and the wickedest man ever I knew."

Claude sniffed. He had heard a lot of hard-luck stories. "Now, your mama wouldn't let you marry him if he was that bad."

"Aye, but he was canny, Mr. Duval. He was darlin' enough at first, until we landed in this country. Then he'd take a dram or two and get to behavin' rather droll. The first time he got drunk, I'm sure he knocked me scatterin', but I repaid him with a shovel when he went to sleep that night. From that hour it was a constant battle between us, but anyway, he's dead now, and I would just as soon not talk about him."

"All right," Claude said, looking over his shoulder. "Let's talk about Ike Lafferty. What made you think he was the one who ransacked your place?"

She turned to him and put her wet hands over the curves of her hips. "I cannot talk about him without talkin' about my husband again. Is it your purpose to torture me with his memory?"

He glanced into the dark. "I know my timing's bad, Correen, but I need to know. Lafferty is a stranger to me. I don't know if I can trust him or not."

"Nor do I," she said, turning back to her dishes. "He argued with my husband every time he came around here, and they threatened each other with every manner of unpleasantry. That's why I suspected him at first, but I don't think he had anything to do with it now."

"I didn't hear you apologize to him."

"Nor will you."

He fought back a smile. "Have you ever heard of an outfit called the Snowy Range Gang?"

"Only rumors."

"Ever seen any outlaws around here?"

She tilted her head and smirked at him. "Not unless I'm lookin' at one right now." Her eyes darted to the twin revolvers.

He grinned, pulled his watch from his pocket, and turned it to catch the lantern light.

"Are you takin' medicine?" she asked. "You've pulled that watch from your vest a dozen times since you landed here."

"Waitin' for my next dose of whiskey," he said. "One swallow on the half hour keeps a man healthy and sober."

"I admire your temperance." She clanged some tin plates together and shoved them into a box in the wagon. "I would admire more your abstinence."

Claude grunted and put his hat on. "I would appreciate it if you didn't tell Lafferty I was askin' about him."

"I have no plans to speak to him," she said.

He nodded and touched his brim. "Good night."

"Till the morn."

He walked to his tent and uncorked his whiskey flask. He tried to concentrate on the case at hand, Lone Wolf Wolverton, Ike Lafferty, the Snowy Range Gang. But instead he caught himself wondering if Correen would stay on in this country now that her husband had been murdered and her sheep herd wiped out. He wouldn't mind looking in on her every now and then.

"There you go again," he heard Dusty say. He felt him there, a faceless presence. "When are you gonna learn, boy? That girl could hog-tie you with a spiderweb right now if she wanted to."

Six

C orreen woke the men before dawn for breakfast. Her hair was washed, combed, and tied back in a twisted, shining bundle. Claude gathered that she had done some shopping for herself in Laramie. She wore a new riding skirt, a white blouse tied at the throat with a black ribbon, and a new pair of leather riding boots buttoned up to her calves.

The stars were still in the sky when she served the bacon and biscuits, the clouds having drifted away. Yesterday's dark cavern of no return had vanished.

After breakfast, Claude stropped his razor and whipped some shaving soap in a bowl of rainwater. He watched Correen as he took his whiskers off. She was getting ready to go somewhere. Not too far away, he hoped. She happened to walk by and glance at him as he was rinsing his face. The other men were striking tents, packing mules.

"Your sideburns are lopsided," she said, shaking her head.

He felt them with his fingertips. "Feel straight to me."

She took the razor from him, flipped the blade from the handle, and compared the two sides of his face. "You shouldn't be shavin' if you don't have a lookin' glass."

He felt her small hand grab his jaw and wrench his head to one side. The blade made two swipes at the left sideburn. She twisted his neck the other way, and he heard the razor scrape the right side of his face in short, hard strokes.

"There now," she said, swizzling the blade in the bowl of water. "That squared it up. Now I won't have to look at crooked sideburns all day." She slapped the folded razor in his hand.

As she walked away, Claude rubbed the tender skin she had scraped. "What do you mean all day?" he said. "We're fixin' to ride up after those outlaws."

She whirled and pierced him with a glare. "And I'll be ridin' with you."

Claude threw the razor into the bowl of water. "Like hell you will. That's a wild outfit we're going after up there."

Bob Steck came to the regulator's side.

"I've got a hired boy and a flock of sheep in those mountains," she said. "I'll not stay below until I know they're alive and well. I've got to look after what's mine."

"I'll look after it for you," Claude said.

"No, thank you, Mr. Duval. I don't need your help."

"And the last thing I need is a woman to look after."

Steck slapped him on the shoulder. "Wyoming gives 'em the vote and they think they can wear britches!" He laughed loudly.

Correen marched to her wagon and drew her Winchester from a leather scabbard. "Have you still got that empty cartridge?" she asked.

Claude patted his vest pocket. "Yeah," he said, puzzled.

She cocked the rifle. "Throw it just as high as you please above your head, Mr. Duval." She put the stock against her cheek.

Taking the big casing from his pocket, Claude smirked at Steck and sent the shell arching against the pale blue sky. Correen swept her barrel in pursuit and squeezed off a shot that twisted her with its recoil. The brass shell angled up and away, whirling, singing through the air. Steck hollered with joy and bounded across the ground to retrieve the target.

"I can look after myself," Correen said. She ejected the smoking shell, chambered a live one, savagely wrenching the lever of the Winchester. She let the hammer down, plucked a fresh cartridge from a box in the wagon, and re-filled the magazine before replacing the rifle in its scabbard.

"Who taught you to shoot like that?" Claude asked.

"My father had an old musket, and I, bein' the oldest, learned to hunt rabbits and deer with it. Only it was poachin' in the old country, and you had to be canny."

Steck strode back with the empty shell, torn open by Correen's shot. "Look at that, Sabinal!" he said joyfully. "I've never seen the likes of it!"

"She still can't go with us."

"Then I'll go alone," she said.

"Aw, let her come along," Steck said. "She's proved she can shoot, and we could use a cook."

"Forget it. Too dangerous. She's not comin'."

Claude had his knee braced against a mule, taking the slack out of a diamond hitch, when he heard Correen ride out. He watched her trot away on her black pony, her spare horse carrying a small pack, expertly secured. When she got to the rise above her homestead, she turned west, toward the mountains.

Steck laughed. "She don't take you serious, Sabinal!"

Ike Lafferty sighed and rolled his eyes.

Claude saddled Casino and chased her half a mile before he caught up. "I told you it was too dangerous for you!" he shouted, standing Casino broadside in front of her on the trail.

She simply reined her mount onto rockier ground and went around the regulator, ignoring him.

He stood there after she passed, cussing her persistence. At last, he loped up the trail and overtook her again.

"All right," he said, "if you're determined to come along, you might as well ride with us where I can keep an eye on you." He wasn't totally against her going, though he suspected she would be more trouble than she was worth.

"No, thank you, Mr. Duval," she said, almost

smiling at him. "I'd rather go on alone." She urged her mare up the trail.

"Dang it, Correen. Wait for the rest of us, I said!"

She pulled her reins and turned in the saddle. "Ask me," she said, her voice almost purring.

"What?"

"Ask me nicely."

Claude groaned. "Will you *please* wait on the rest of us?" He was thankful that Steck and Lafferty weren't listening, but knew Dusty was, and heard the echo of his partner's laughter.

"Well," she said, letting her eyelids sag as she felt her bundle of hair for loose strands, "I'm sure I might wait if you'd hurry along." She reined her mare under a pine and hopped down from the saddle.

"You have no idea what kind of a mess you're gettin' into," he said.

She glanced at him over her shoulder as she loosened the saddle girth. "And you, Mr. Duval, have no idea what kind of messes I have overcome long before I met you."

Correen grilled the men for information as the pack train moved slowly into the forests of fir, pine, and spruce that covered the high country.

"Sacred cattle in the sacred mountains," she remarked.

Steck was riding beside her, enjoying her conversation. "What do you mean by that?" he asked.

"Little Crow, my shepherd boy, has told me his people's lore of these mountains. He's from the Ute tribe. His people once came to these mountains to get wood for makin' bows, and to make 'medicine' as he calls it: magic." Her green eyes flared at mention of the word. "That's how these became known as the Medicine Bow Mountains. They are sacred to the Ute people, and now you have come for your sacred cattle here."

"How'd you come by a Ute boy?" Claude asked, looking back at her, resting his hand on the cantle as he rode. "I thought they were all on reservations."

"They were going to send Little Crow to school and make him learn English. His father thought bad of it and urged him to run away. I found him a year ago in the mountains, fed him, and put him to work with the sheep."

"How do you get along with him if he don't speak English?" Steck said.

"I know a few words of Ute, and he a few of English. And he has taught me some of the hand signs. We communicate well enough."

They rounded a bend in the trail, Claude pausing to admire a small mountain brook running along the edge of a meadow. Beavers had dammed it, forming a small lake. "We'll stop here to have lunch and let the horses graze," he said.

"I'll bet it's full of trout," Correen said, smiling at him as if she had come for a holiday picnic.

As the other men went for firewood, Claude walked around the pond to scout for signs of deer, elk, and rustlers. He looked across the water and saw the reflections of the horses in the still water. He liked what he saw here. Dusty sure knew how to pick a ranch site. Mountains, plains, foothills, and Correen all within a day's ride.

He caught Correen looking at him across the pond and turned his eyes to the ground again. He was trying not to think of her as available. One of the bad habits he had learned to temper over the years concerned women. "A pretty girl can knock you over with an eyelash," Dusty had once told him. In the past, various members of the gender had stolen Claude's heart, money, pride, or combinations of the three. He had trained himself to watch for deceptions. He hadn't found any in Correen yet, but wasn't about to let himself get taken in by her looks or her lilting talk.

And, after all, the woman's husband had just died. Even if she did hate the man, she wasn't going to be in a hurry to replace him. But could she ever be interested in a black sheep like Claude Duval? He would have to proceed carefully with her. He knew his weaknesses. He was still feeling her firm grip on his clean-shaven jaw.

He risked another glance at her, caught her removing something from a long tube on her packhorse. Putting sticks together now, end-to-end. Stringing them with . . . Thread? What the . . . ? A damned fishing pole? Yes, a crank reel fixed to the handle.

He stormed back around the pond, but by the time he jumped the brook below the beaver dam, she had her line played out, flicking it gracefully out over the water and back over her shoulder. He stopped to watch her for a moment, fascinated. Never had he seen such fishing, flogging the surface of the water like a stage driver flicking the rump of a horse.

"Woman, what in the name of the devil do you think you're doin'?" he growled.

"Angling, Mr. Duval. I've brought along my new pole I ordered from—"

"Do you think this is a damned pleasure trip?" he said, interrupting her. "Do you think we've got time to . . ." His eyes got stuck on the end of the line that kept whipping over her shoulder. "What are you usin' for bait?"

"A wee bucktail fly," she said, letting the end of the line light finally, her alert eyes staying with it.

"A fly?"

"I'm sure I never said it wasn't. Now, stand back if you will, sir, or you'll frighten our lunch away."

"Correen, if you catch a fish with a fly, I'll . . ."

The surface of the pond erupted in a spout of water and a glint of scales. The angler snapped her rod back, bending it, and began taking line up on her reel. "You'll what, Mr. Duval? Have it for lunch?"

Claude stared in stupefaction as she played the trout to the shore and into her waiting hand. He looked over her shoulder as she removed the hook, a tiny bend of steel with bits of feather and hair tied to it. "Well, I'll be damned," he said. "That's not a bad fish."

"Past the common," she replied, handing the catch to him. "You might as well start guttin'."

As they ate their fresh fried trout, Claude laid down the rules for the rest of the expedition. "No shootin', except in self-defense. I don't want any hollerin', whistlin', or loud talkin'. Don't do anything that might spook the horses. Correen, keep the cook fires small, and douse 'em as soon as possible after dark. We don't know how close they are, so we'll start takin' turns at guard duty tonight. That means you, too, Correen."

She tried to respond, but he had purposefully caught her with her mouth full.

"Remember, if Wolverton's up here with 'em, he can blow a hole in any one of us from four hundred yards. Maybe farther. That means we have to watch a circle a half mile across all the time. You see where you're sittin' right now, Bob?"

"Huh?" Steck said, looking at the ground under him.

"You're liable to get Lone-Wolfed right there. Wolverton has a clean shot at your back from that ridge yonder, right at three hundred yards. He likes to take 'em in the back."

The Texan craned his neck, looked wild-eyed at the ridge behind him, picked up his plate, and found a safer place against a tree.

"Ike," the regulator said, "have you got any idea where this gang might be holed up?"

The rancher had finished eating and was whittling a soft piece of pine. "Not really. There's hundreds of hidin' places in these mountains."

"How do you aim to find 'em, Sabinal, with no tracks to follow?" Steck asked.

"First thing we need to worry about is findin' Correen's Indian boy. After we find him, we'll scout the ridges and look for campfire smoke. Correen, where you reckon that boy is?"

"He'll be near the Snowy Range this time of

year. He's expectin' me to bring his supplies in a few days. He'll be easy enough to find."

"Just pray that Wolverton's gang doesn't find him before we do." He slung a fish spine from his plate, pulled his watch from his pocket, and smiled. "You gentlemen care for an after-dinner drink?"

Late in the afternoon, Claude led his party over a ridge and got his first look at the Snowy Range through a gap in the trees. The row of rocky peaks jutted above the timberline, bathed in sunlight, streaked with year-round snow. He felt compelled to ride over and see them, but knew they were farther away than they looked through the thin alpine air.

"We'll camp down in this draw," he said. "Looks like we'll make the Snowy Range by tomorrow afternoon." He let the pack train file by him and stayed on the ridge to admire the barren pinnacles. As he tried to take it all in, the breeze and the sweet Scottish lilt chilled him so that he almost shivered.

"Beautiful, isn't it?" Correen said.

Claude grunted, allowing himself a glimpse of her face.

"Reminds me of the Highlands of home."

"It looks like this over there?"

"A bit tamer, I'm sure."

He gripped his saddle horn. "A tamer country's a good place for a woman on her own."

"I have no desire to go back now, Mr. Duval. I have come to love it here and will love it all the more now that my husband is dead. I only need to get my horses back and punish those who slaughtered my sheep."

"Without gettin' killed," Claude added. She's going to stay, he thought. That's good, but this ain't the time to think about it. Wolverton's out there somewhere. Hell, for all you know, she begged Lone Wolf to kill her husband. She may be in it with him. You've been fooled by pretty faces before, boy. Watch yourself.

"You haven't told us everything, have you?" she said.

He tried to look dumbfounded. "Huh?"

"You're following their trail, and you haven't told Mr. Steck and Mr. Lafferty."

"What trail?" Claude said. "The rain's washed all the tracks away."

"And beaten down the heaps of horse and cattle dung, but they're still underfoot of us."

Claude couldn't prevent his eyebrows from raising. "Anybody's stock could have left that sign. Lafferty runs cattle up here."

"Aye, but this sign runs a straight path. They were movin' slow, lettin' the sacred cattle graze. The grass they cropped is still plain to see. And don't think I didn't spot their campfire ashes at the pond."

Claude smiled in spite of himself. "Where'd you learn to read sign like that?"

"Trailin' my flocks, huntin' food. Little Crow teaches me something new every time I see him."

"Well, don't let on to Bob and Ike that we're on the trail of those outlaws."

"Why not?"

"Because Bob flies off the handle, and I don't know what Lafferty is liable to do. I don't want them gettin' nervous till the last minute."

She nodded. "There's still something you're

not telling us, Mr. Duval. I'd say you're more than a hired detective to this shootin' party. You've got something personal at stake."

Claude scoffed and looked away. "What gave you that kind of idea?"

"There's sign to read on the ground, Mr. Duval, then there's that in a man's eyes. I see blood in yours."

Her keen stare stayed with him even after she rode down to the campsite. He pulled his watch from his pocket. Still twelve minutes shy of the hour. "Damn," he said.

Seven

❧

Claude picked up his Marlin repeater as he left camp. "Bob, you'll relieve me at nine o'clock. Correen, put the fire out as soon as you get through with it." He looked at Lafferty, who was leaning against a tree, whittling. "You better turn in early, Ike. You'll stand morning guard."

He walked to a slope overlooking the camp and sat down against a tree trunk, relieved to be beyond the eyes of his campmates. The pistol grip of the Marlin felt good in his palm. He could sort things out up here.

Bob Steck? Not afraid to fight. The trouble was holding him back until the fight started.

Ike Lafferty? Quiet. Calm. But he's got a temper. Showed that back at his ranch. Correen doesn't like him, and she's a good judge. Agreeable enough so far, but watch him.

And what about Correen? Can't control her.

Does what she pleases. Good hand around camp, but she's trouble. A woman is always trouble.

He looked at the stars over the Snowy Range and remembered the nights he and Dusty rode night-herd together on the trail. One would circle the herd to the right, the other to the left, and Dusty always had something funny to say every time they crossed paths. Claude was young then, felt old now.

He sat against his tree for an hour, until a peal of Bob Steck's laughter caught his attention. He shook his head in disgust when he saw the campfire burning brightly. He figured he'd better go back and lay down the law.

"Correen!" he said, stepping from the shadows. "I told you to put that fire out! And you, Bob, I can hear you laughin' half a mile from camp! This ain't no damn pleasure trip!"

He propped his Marlin against a saddle and began kicking dirt on the fire. Dust and smoke filled the air as the light dwindled. But before the last tongues of fire could die, Claude sensed something near. Looking up, he glimpsed an image across the smoking wood that jolted him with a pang of terror.

A form emerged from the shadows, swaggering through the smoke and dust. He saw the dull glint of a weapon and the glare of the eyes under the dark brim. The face came clear, a sunken version of an old nightmare. It rode a lank human frame that skulked silently in among the campers and towered over them.

Claude tried to get his revolver out of the holster but found the rifle barrel of the intruder covering him.

"Don't do it," the voice said. It was so low that it almost croaked, and it rattled an old chord of hatred in the pit of Claude's heart. "I don't mean to harm anybody." His black hair was cropped short, barely sticking out under his hat.

Bob Steck sprang to his feet and stepped in front of Correen. "What the hell do you mean, wadin' into our camp gun-first?"

The eyes, sparkling in their narrow slots, darted to every member of the party, then lingered on Claude. "Take it easy. I don't want any trouble. I'm lookin' for a gentleman named Bob Steck, of Texas. I have a letter for him." He pulled an envelope from his coat pocket.

"I'm Steck."

The big man continued to guard Claude as he handed the envelope to Steck. He squinted again at the regulator. "You look familiar."

"You've got a good memory," Claude said. "You only laid eyes on me once before. You've taken off a lot of weight since I saw you last."

"Hard labor," the visitor said.

"You two know each other?" Steck asked, tearing open the envelope.

"This is the man we came up here after," Claude said. "This is Lone Wolf Wolverton."

Ike Lafferty dropped the piece of wood he had been whittling and got to his feet.

"I'm not the man you're after," Wolverton said. "That letter will prove it."

Steck was trying to make out the writing. "I can't see a damn thing. Correen, what does it say?"

She took the letter from Steck and knelt by the fire to catch the light. Claude's temper flared when he saw Wolverton's eyes look her up and down.

"Dear Bob . . ." Her accent attracted another glance from the rifleman. "A gentleman known as Lone Wolf Wolverton has taken up residence near me and engaged in agriculture. I have seen him every day on his farm since he located here and know he could have had no part in the recent crimes occurring on your ranch. The Texas Rangers have investigated him and found him faultless. I know Mr. Wolverton as a good neighbor and churchgoer. Kindest regards, Bill Johnson."

"Bill Johnson!" Steck said, taking the letter back from Correen. "That's an old friend of mine, Sabinal. His word's good."

"You could have forced anybody to write that," Claude said to Wolverton. "Anyway, why would you travel across half the country to deliver it?"

"I'm after those outlaws, like the rest of you."

"Why?"

"They're tryin' to make it look like I'm with 'em."

"Why would they do that?"

"Maybe to put the blame on me. Maybe to scare posses off their trail. Either way, I can't allow it."

Claude sneered at the big man, his anger building. "I say you *are* with 'em. Your empty cartridges keep turnin' up in the hands of dead men."

"I don't even own a Creedmoor now. I give you my word."

"Your word doesn't mean shit to me, Wolverton."

The big man frowned and glowered at Claude. "Where do I know you from?"

He met Wolverton's stare, turned it back. "I'm Dusty Sanderson's partner."

Wolverton's eyes widened, and his jaw dropped.

"Who the hell is Dusty Sanderson?" Steck blurted.

"Tell him," Claude said to Wolverton. "I want to hear *you* explain it."

Wolverton's stare dropped to the ground. "He was the man I went to prison for killin'. I mistook him for a rustler I was after name of Giff Dearborn."

"Mistake, hell. You murdered him," Claude said.

"I gave a guilty plea. I owned up to what I did and paid for it."

"You haven't paid squat. You're still breathin' and Dusty's still dead. I was the one who found him, Wolverton. Shot in the back. A hole through him big as my fist. That cartridge shell in his hand. His face burned off where your bullet knocked him into the fire, and you just left him there."

The glistening eyes looked up at Claude again. "Now I remember you. The courtroom, the day the judge sentenced me."

"I should have killed you then," Claude said. "I had the gun in my pocket."

"Things are different now. I've changed."

Claude chuckled. "Yeah, I see you have. You've gone from regulatin' to rustlin'."

"Why would I barge into your camp if that was true? I came here to clear myself with Mr. Steck and to help him catch those rustlers."

"He's talkin' sense, Sabinal. He could have already shot you."

Wolverton's eyes caught another flash of surprise. "Sabinal? Are you Claude Duval?"

"I am."

"I've met a dozen men you sent to prison. By golly, I never knew Dusty was partners with Sabinal Claude."

Claude quivered with rage. "You dare speak his name like you knew him! Goddamn you, Wolverton! First chance I get, you're a dead man!"

Wolverton sighed and set his jaw. "I don't think so," he said.

"Try me."

"Oh, I know you'd do it. But not tonight. Not here. A gunshot might bring those outlaws down on your camp. You've got to think of your friends. Especially the woman. I know your reputation, Duval. You're a fair man. You'll wait." As he stared into Claude's pale eyes, he raised the barrel of his rifle to the sky and eased the hammer down to the safety position. Then he lowered the rifle butt to the ground and put his hand on the muzzle.

Claude snatched a big Russian from his right-hand holster.

"No!" Correen cried.

"Don't do it, Sabinal," Steck warned. "Wolverton's right. We don't want to stampede them outlaws."

Claude felt his hand trembling, hoped it didn't show. He had sworn long ago that if he ever got this chance, nothing would stop him. But he hadn't counted on circumstances like these. He fought the urge to jerk the trigger, and lowered his revolver. "Get the hell out of my sight, Wolverton."

"Wait," Lafferty said, stepping forward. "I don't trust him out there with that rifle. I'd rather he stay in camp where we can watch him. He says he's after the same rustlers we're after. Let's give him a chance to prove it."

Claude thought for a few seconds, then nodded. "You may have somethin' there, Ike." He put his revolver in the holster and picked up his Marlin. "All right, Wolverton, bring your gear in. But, like you said, I'm a fair man, so I'll give you advance warnin'. As soon as we take care of this Snowy Range Gang, you'd better make yourself scarce if you want a chance to live." He stalked back into the dark to take his guard.

Eight

~∞~

She came up behind him, silently, while he was shaving. "Do you know why they tremble so?" she asked.

Claude flinched, felt the blade nick him, turned to upbraid her for sneaking in on him. But she was looking at the fluttering leaves of the quaking aspens, her eyes reflecting their tremulous energy, and he couldn't speak harshly to her. "Huh?"

"Little Crow says the leaves tremble at the passing of the wind god. The trees must show their fear, or the wind god will tear their limbs asunder." She broke off a small branch with about a dozen leaves on it.

Claude smiled, his face half covered with shaving soap. "You believe in that sort of thing?"

"I might if I didn't study things so." She

plucked a single leaf and held it in front of his face. "The stem is flat, with a quarter twist. You would tremble, too, if you had to stand like that in the wind." She swept her aspen branch gracefully over her head, its leaves fluttering through the cool morning air.

"You just took the wind out of a thousand years of Indian legend."

She shrugged and tossed the branch carelessly aside. "I believe what I see, Mr. Duval."

Claude took another swipe at his chin with the razor. "What were you talkin' to Lone Wolf about this mornin'?" He had seen the gaunt man towering over her as she cooked, and it had bothered him.

"Just talkin'. He's a nice man to talk to."

"Correen, I know you don't like me tellin' you what to do, but I advise you to keep your distance from that man. He'd shoot you in the back if somebody'd pay him to do it, and never give it a second thought."

"Strange," she answered. "That's not at all the sort of thing he said about you this mornin'."

"What?"

She lifted his chin with her finger and studied his neck. "He said you were a fine man. Tough but fair. Brave, honest, and bound by the law." She took the towel from Claude's shoulder and dabbed at his throat. "You cut yourself," she said, showing him the blood.

"You believe what he says?" Claude took the towel from her and held it against his cut.

"I don't believe either one of you any more than I believe the leaves tremble before the wind god. I believe what I see." She tossed her brown hair as she turned, and went to pack her gear.

Claude finished shaving, wondering how Wolverton had managed to make him look bad by saying good things about him. He put his shaving kit in his saddlebag with the Le Mat revolver and reached for the gun belt holding the twin Russians.

As he buckled the belt around his hips, he caught Wolverton staring at him. "What're you lookin' at?" he said.

"Your hardware. What do you carry all that weight for?"

"The likes of you."

Ike Lafferty led a packhorse between them. "I'm no gunman," he said, patting his Peacemaker, "but I thought Colt built the best weapon. What do you see in those Smiths?"

"Solid weapon," Claude said, drawing the right-hand one. "Good balance." He put his thumb under the rear sight and lifted the latch, breaking the revolver open. The action kicked all six rounds out at once into his waiting palm. "Reloads faster than that gate-loader you're wearin'."

Lafferty nodded thoughtfully.

"If you can't hit what you're shootin' at with twelve rounds," Wolverton said, "reloading won't do you much good."

Claude snapped the empty revolver shut and pointed it at Wolverton, cocking it, looking down the sights at the bridge of the big man's nose. "I've never shot more than one at a time into a man. Never had to. I might use a dozen or more on you, though. Just for fun." He pulled the trigger and let the hammer fall on an empty cylinder.

Wolverton sighed. "You'd give that idea up if you'd been where I've been."

"I don't care where you've been. Just where you're goin'. Straight to hell, and it's my job to send you there."

Wolverton frowned and turned away, shaking his head.

After replacing the six live rounds, Claude looked up and saw Correen staring at him, arms crossed like a schoolmarm about to scold a rowdy pupil. He felt ridiculous. He had never used such reckless talk in his life, and now she had to be on hand to hear it. But his beef with Wolverton went back long before he ever laid eyes on Correen. He wasn't going to let Lone Wolf get away alive to please a woman he hardly knew. He had to think of Dusty.

When they took to the trail, Correen rode up past the pack mules, pacing Claude once she reached the head of the string.

"I wanted to kill Mr. Galloway sure as you've got it in for Mr. Wolverton," she said. "I swore I'd do it the next time he raised his hand to me. I was lucky. Someone else came along and did the killin' for me, else I'd burn in hell for murder."

"Hell?" Claude said, raking his long hair back. "I thought you only believed in things you've seen."

"I'm sure I've seen my share," she said. And they rode on together in silence.

Nine

∽◦∽

The three riders came over the Medicine Bow Divide, past the scrubby wind-twisted evergreens, over the tundralike graze. The peaks of the Snowy Range loomed five miles to their left. Only Strikes the Dog looked at the rock pinnacles jutting skyward above the trees like the jagged edges of a broken pot left out in the snow. Behind her, the black man and the gang leader were too busy talking to take notice.

"One: Lone Wolf Wolverton gets pardoned out of prison. Two: This fellow Steck comes back from India with all them bremmer cattle. Three: Wild Roy Wiloughby puts 'em together and makes history for cattle rustlin'."

It was Wild Roy himself talking—short, ugly, face like an old plow pitted with rust. To Strikes the Dog his face resembled the cratered surface of the moon, and she thought of him as Moon

Face, though she never called him that out loud. Never spoke to him at all, in fact.

The only one in the gang she spoke to was the black one, the one the others called Squaw Man. He was her man—to sleep with, to cook for. He protected her from the others: Moon Face and the two red-haired brothers—the evil twins, like two humans sharing a single soul.

She hated all these white men. She cursed them for coming back to her mountains. When she was a girl, the white men had poisoned her brother's mind with firewater. Poisoned him to the point that he sold her to the soldiers at the fort to get more money for more firewater. Now they simply called her Squaw, but she knew she was Strikes the Dog, and the name was medicine to her wounds.

"How do you know about them cattle sweatin' poison and all?" Squaw Man said, tilting his cavalry cap on his head. He was bearded with dense curls, always sleepy-eyed except in a fight. He was still trying to get all the details about the bremmers out of Wild Roy. They hadn't had much time to talk since Laramie.

"I heard Steck braggin' on 'em in a saloon down in Texas. Damn fool all but told me how to steal 'em. Just had one man guardin' 'em, quarantined on Matagorda Island." He patted the stock of the long rifle in his saddle boot. "Figured I'd better get a old Sharps Creedmoor like Lone Wolf used to use if I was gonna make it look like him. Couldn't find one, though, so you know what I did?"

"No."

"I tracked down Lone Wolf's old rifle. Yeah, found out a judge up in the Panhandle had kept it after Lone Wolf's trial, so I broke into the judge's house and stolt it. Anyway, once I had the Creedmoor, I shot a fellow owned a little steamboat. Put that shell in his hand like Wolverton always done. Took the boat to Matagorda Island, killed the cowboy guardin' the bremmers, and herded 'em onto the steamboat. Sailed up into Lavaca Bay, let the cattle rest a day till dark, then herded 'em twenty miles overnight to the depot at Telferner."

"Reckon they're missin' them cattle yet?"

"Don't give a damn if they are. They'll be lookin' for Wolverton down there. Time they figure out he didn't do it, it'll be too late to trail me."

"How do you know this Wolverton ain't comin' after you?"

Wiloughby laughed. "Preacher Wolverton? He'll stay put in Texas. Prison took all the killin' out of him. Used to read the Gospel to us Sundays."

"You listen to any of it?"

"Hell, yes. Sunday school got you out of chores."

They rode silently into a line of trees, passing the white trunks of aspens, mottled with black scars.

Squaw Man was worried. Without Roy Wiloughby, life had been hard but enjoyable for the past year and a half. It had been just him and the squaw, living off the land in the Medicine Bows.

He had come to the mountains three years ago, on the run for killing a smart-mouthed sutler at Fort Casper. The squaw was a Fort Casper whore he had brought with him. Up near the

Snowy Range, he had stumbled onto Wiloughby and the Sickle twins, Clay and Frank, driving a herd of stolen beeves. He and his squaw had helped the outlaws move the cattle, earning an uneasy trust.

"What do we call you?" Wild Roy had said, the day he took the former buffalo soldier into the Snowy Range Gang.

"I ain't tellin' my name."

"Shit, I ain't gonna shoot you for bounty."

"I said I ain't tellin'."

"Damn, you're a spooky squaw man."

It had seemed like a good thing a couple of years ago, raiding the ranches to the north, selling the cattle in Colorado. Then Wild Roy and the Sickle twins had gone to Texas for a tear, landed in prison for a year for stealing a saddle. Squaw Man had found that he and his woman could get along all right in the mountains on their own—hunting, trapping, living in a tepee, avoiding civilization.

He went to Laramie once or twice a year for supplies, and there he had found a letter, sent care of the outfitter the Snowy Range Gang had always done business with. It was from Roy Wiloughby: "Out of prison in Texas. Wait for me early September, Big Hollow."

Now the gang was back together, and Squaw Man wasn't so sure he liked it. Imported cattle rustled from a rich Texas rancher, using the sign of a bloody ex-regulator. Could be trouble, but he would go along with it. He always went along with Wild Roy for some reason. He didn't know why. He didn't really like the son of a bitch.

"How'd you get them bremmers on the train with nobody seein' 'em?" Squaw Man asked.

"I knew the foreman at Telferner. Paid him to keep quiet. Clay and Frank helped me put 'em on in the middle of the night, and we was on our way north."

Squaw Man shook his head. "Somebody seen them cattle between here and Texas. Had to."

"I hope they did. I hope they know I took 'em. I never heard tell of nobody rustlin' no cattle like that. I hope they put my name in the paper."

Squaw Man frowned. "That fellow Steck gonna come lookin'?"

"That old bastard? Hell, no. He might hire some detectives, but they'll go after Wolverton first. Time they figure out he didn't do it, we'll have them bremmers scattered all over the territory. Then we'll split up for the winter, spend all our money, get back together next spring."

Squaw Man grunted. Wild Roy thought he was some outlaw. Damn fool was going to get them all lynched one day.

Strikes the Dog's Indian pony crunched tracks in a patch of snow that hadn't seen sunlight all summer. She couldn't hear the forest very well over the clopping hooves of the trotting horses and the squeaking saddle leather. But she could see and smell. She knew they were getting close.

Suddenly, she jerked her horse to a stop as the men came up beside her. She made a few fluid signs, mostly with her right hand.

"She smells 'em," Squaw Man said. "Maybe two miles upwind."

"The hell," Wiloughby said. "Sheep stink, but that squaw can't smell 'em two miles."

"She says remind you not to kill the boy."

"Why don't she tell me herself? She talks to you. What the hell does she want with that boy, anyway?"

"I keep him," Strikes the Dog said, answering Wiloughby, but looking at Squaw Man. "He work."

"The boy's Ute," Squaw Man explained. "The Cheyenne used to catch Ute boys and adopt 'em. Make 'em slaves first, then turn 'em into braves."

Wiloughby looked at the woman. "He causes me trouble one time, I'll kill him." He knew she understood, though she ignored him. "Hell, maybe he'll make a rustler. At least he can carry water, chop wood."

Strikes the Dog slacked her reins and kicked her pony, leading the men into the wind, across a meadow, then winding through the trees, ducking branches. They went quietly, at a walk. After a mile, the bleating of sheep reached them through the forest.

"Goddamn stinkin' woollies," the gang leader said. "Listen at 'em."

Roy Wiloughby hated sheep. They took range from cattle, and he couldn't stand to think of rustling sheep someday, the cattle all pressed out of the country. He hated the way they smelled, though he wasn't fond of the scent of cattle, either. He hated their cowardly little voices, their stupidity, their bug eyes.

The only thing he liked about sheep was killing them. Sheep and sheep people, he had found, were usually easy targets. The animals would bunch together when threatened, where they could be easily shot, or clubbed if he didn't want to waste ammunition. And shepherds often worked alone, far from the law.

Coming over a timbered ridge, they saw glimpses of wool below, through the trees, sunlit in a meadow. The bleating voices came clearer.

"Look like a bunch of goddamn maggots," Wiloughby said.

"How you wanna do it?" Squaw Man asked quietly.

"Give your squaw a few minutes to sneak close to the boy. Then . . ." He stroked his thinly bearded jaw, trying to look thoughtful. "There a bluff close to here?"

Squaw Man pointed. "About half a mile that way. Seventy-, eighty-foot drop."

"We'll rimrock 'em, by God. Always wanted to try that. But first I'll limber up ol' Creed. Gotta keep the eye in." He squinted his left eye, rolling the right one. Grinning, he pulled the Creedmoor from the saddle boot, stroked the stock. "You still a bettin' man?"

The black man shrugged. "What's the bet?"

"A hundred dollars says ol' Creed will shoot through three sheep with one shot."

"I reckon she might," Squaw Man said, "you line 'em up just right, hit 'em through the guts."

"How 'bout four?"

"You got a bet." He shook the little white man's hand.

Strikes the Dog rode north to get around the meadow and find the Ute boy she wanted to capture. Wiloughby and Squaw Man went south, got below the meadow, and dismounted in the timber. They snuck toward the clearing until they could see the hundred grazing sheep, their woolly backs undulating like a giant living rug.

They heard the sheepdog bark, then a pistol shot and a yelp. The woman burst into the meadow at a gallop and they saw the Indian boy running for cover, the squaw pouncing on him from the saddle. Sheep scattered in a moment of panic, then bunched in the middle of the clearing. The Creedmoor roared, hazing the air with black powder smoke. The flock surged as one, some sheep jumping over others, a hundred bleats filling the air like the hollering of spoiled children.

"Four down!" Wiloughby shouted, laughing. "Pay up!"

"Let's go see," Squaw Man said, his sleepy eyes turning away from the meadow as he walked for his horse.

They loped into the meadow, found two wounded sheep lying on their sides, gut-shot, heaving, eyes rolling. A third stood on wobbly legs, head hanging, blood dripping from its belly. A fourth butted against the flock, seeking protection, a busted leg dragging.

Squaw Man scattered the flock, reaching low to grab the fourth sheep by the ear. He lifted it and could hear its terrified voice calling his name: "Squaw Maaaaan! Squaw Maaaaan!" He dropped the poor beast, unnerved. He had been living like an Indian too long. The animals were talking to him.

"You owe me a hundred," Wiloughby said.

"That fourth one's not shot through," Squaw Man replied.

"I said ol' Creed would hit four with one shot."

"You said you'd shoot *through* four. You pay *me*."

"Bullshit, boy. I'll take a hundred out of your cut when we sell the rest of them bremmers."

Squaw Man was riled, his eyes showing it, wide with anger. He rode toward Wiloughby, his hand on his pistol butt. "Won't do you no good dead."

Wild Roy laughed. "You gonna kill me over a hundred dollars?"

"Call me boy again, I'll kill you for that."

"Oh, goddamn," the little white man said, rolling his eyes. "Bet's off. You didn't make yourself clear. Shoot all the way through four sheep, hell. Which way is that bluff?"

Squaw Man tilted his head, keeping his eyes on Wiloughby.

The little man pressed the flock toward the bluff. "Come on, let's rimrock these little pill-shitters."

They passed Strikes the Dog, kneeling on the squirming Ute boy's back, tying his hands behind him with a rawhide thong. Squaw Man shook his head at the strangeness of the sight. A squaw and a longhaired boy, both in white men's clothing, thrashing the ground in their struggle.

They reached the bluff after a short stampede and pressed the surging body of sheep toward the rim. The leaders reached the drop-off, balked, then tried to back up or turn around. But Wiloughby drew his pistol and fired into the air, hollering and whistling at the sheep. The animals in back pressed frantically against the leaders, forcing them over the brink.

Squaw Man heard the blatting voices fade as

they fell. Then the bodies of the animals began to thud against the rocks below. He worked with Wiloughby, pushing the sheep toward the rim. They followed the leaders almost willingly now, leaping into thin air, somersaulting as they plummeted. He heard Wiloughby laughing with joy, impact jolting dying blats from the sheep. He wished Wild Roy had stayed in Texas. The dying sheep were calling his name again: "Squaw Maaaan! Squaw Maaaan!"

Ten

❧

Little Crow stumbled along at a trot behind the Cheyenne woman's horse, his hands bound behind him, the rawhide noose tightening around his neck whenever he tried to slow down. He knew he was alone in this. The squaw had pounced on him from one of Correen's horses. He figured Correen and her mean drunk of a husband for dead. He expected no rescue.

He had seen sign of Squaw Man and Strikes the Dog in the mountains before, spotted them once from a distance. But they had always let him alone. It seemed the little ugly white man had caused them to kill his sheep and take him captive. He was scared but hoped his face didn't show it. He wanted this Cheyenne woman to know he was a brave Ute.

He was trying to act more exhausted than he really was. If they thought he had nothing left to run with, they would ease their guard on him, and he could try to escape. But they had already dragged him past the Snowy Range, across the divide to the western slopes. Sharp rocks had bruised his feet through his moccasins. He had fallen three times on the trail, and the ground had scraped a shoulder and a cheek raw. The squaw could have dragged him and choked him to death, but she didn't want to kill him. Not yet, anyway.

The trail finally led over the rim of a bluff and Little Crow got a glimpse of the gang's camp in a park below. He saw the tepee the black man and Strikes the Dog lived in and the log walls of the cabin the gang had begun to build. Between the unfinished cabin and the tepee, he saw something hanging from a slanting timber, but it disappeared behind treetops before he could make it out.

He staggered down the steep trail behind the squaw's horse until she came to a stream. Strikes the Dog stopped him in the rushing water and turned in the saddle to look at him.

Little Crow was thirsty, so he lowered himself to one knee to put his mouth against the surface of the stream, shin-deep where he had stopped. He was ready for what happened next. The noose tightened around his neck and the cold water engulfed him. Floundering to his feet, he heard the little ugly white man laughing, then the squaw's horse jerked him toward the bank. But he had sucked in a mouthful of water, and that would help.

There was nothing but the cool breeze to dry him, the sun having sunk behind the treetops. But there was plenty of daylight left and Little

Crow knew he would dry before the frigid night came on. He was trying to see his advantages, though they numbered few.

When Strikes the Dog led him into the camp, the boy collapsed as if he couldn't take another step. She untied the leash from her saddle horn and dropped it. He thought for a moment of running but knew it would get him nowhere. He would rest, wait for night, use the darkness to his advantage.

He lay on his side, gasping, taking in his surroundings. The slanting timber between the tepee and the cabin stood nearby—a sweep used to suspend camp meat above the reach of bears and wolves. It consisted of a long pine timber, propped up at an angle on an old tree stump. The stump was four feet high and almost as thick, with a saddle chopped into the top of it to cradle the meat pole. The butt of the pole rested on the ground and had two logs bound to it with rope and rawhide to give it counterweight. Little Crow saw a beef carcass swaying on the tip of the pole but doubted he would get any of it.

The black man rode by him, dismounted, and began stripping the saddle from his horse. The gang leader trotted toward the log walls. Beyond the unfinished cabin, the boy saw the two redheaded brothers coming on their horses, and beyond them, a herd of humped bulls, ghost-colored with sagging ears, staring at him as if they felt sorry for him.

Something hit him in the back, and he looked up to see Strikes the Dog glaring down at him. She had come over just to kick him. He didn't move. She kicked him again and padded silently away on her moccasins.

When he looked toward the white men again, he saw the ugly one coming with an axe and an iron stake, coming right at him, grinning. The boy fought his fear and lay still.

"Squaw Man," Roy Wiloughby said. "You ever heard tell of a Indian runnin' ten, twenty miles and such? This one here looks plumb give out runnin' just six or seven."

Little Crow winced as Wiloughby jabbed the iron stake into the ground in front of his face. With the blunt end of the axe, the gang leader drove the stake pin deep into the ground, the Indian boy hoping the axe wouldn't glance and cave in his skull.

"What are you doin'?" Squaw Man asked.

"Stakin' the little bastard down." He threw the axe aside and pulled Little Crow's face against the stake pin with the rawhide loop. "That's Squaw's boy. She'll train him."

Wiloughby jerked a hard rawhide knot around the stake pin and raised up, his hands propped defiantly on his hips. "I'll stake down whatever I damn well want in my camp."

Squaw Man's frown deepened, but he said nothing. He led his horse toward the pole corral.

Little Crow felt the squaw's toe jab him in the back again and heard Wiloughby's hoarse laughter.

The redheaded twins trotted up and dismounted in unison. They frightened the boy more than the squaw or the ugly gang leader. They didn't menace him, but their every move seemed coordinated, and he knew they had some evil medicine about them that made them look and act so much alike. When they looked at him, their eyes hit him at once.

He heard Strikes the Dog's moccasins turn in the sand behind him and knew she was walking back toward the tepee. With her back turned to them, the eyes of the evil twins rose together and searched her from the ankles up, and back down again. Then they looked at each other and communicated something without speaking. All this Little Crow saw through his squint of false anguish.

He was shivering now, lying on his side on the ground, the tether around his neck tied so short to the stake pin that he couldn't sit up. He had dried from his fall in the creek, but it was still cold. His arms were cramped behind his back, the rawhide cutting his wrists. But he had a plan.

Wiloughby had tied the knot tight around the stake pin, but he hadn't doubled it. Little Crow would wait for dark, then he would begin loosening the knot with his teeth. It might take an hour or more to untie. The axe was still lying where Wiloughby had tossed it aside. He would pick it up on his way out of camp and use it to cut his wrists free. After that he didn't know what he would do, except run.

Strikes the Dog suddenly stepped over him from behind and glared down at him, as if she might have felt him plotting. She had a knife in her hand and Little Crow feared for a second that she might torture him with it, but she walked instead toward the sweep where the beef carcass hung.

She grabbed a rope dangling from the high

end of the sweep and cried, "Squaw Man! Squaw Man!" When the black man looked from the corral, she pointed at the beef hanging above her.

"Frank!" Squaw Man shouted. "You and Clay come help me get some meat down for the squaw."

The Sickle twins threw their tools down at the cabin where they had been notching and laying up logs with Wiloughby. They marched in stride, like soldiers.

It took Squaw Man, Strikes the Dog, and both Sickle twins to lower the meat pole. The gang had made the counterweight heavy enough to keep two or three elk carcasses in the air and still prevent big bears from pulling down on the pole and stealing the camp meat. As they pulled on the rope, the beef descended, the long timber pivoting in its cradle on the stump, the weighted butt lifting unwillingly from the ground.

Little Crow noticed the Sickle twins pressing against the woman harder than the task demanded. He was young and didn't understand completely, but had a vague instinct for what they were doing, and it made him uncomfortable. He didn't want anyone getting the squaw mad, for she would probably take it out on him.

With the beef carcass within reach, Strikes the Dog stood on the rope while the men held it, and carved a section of hindquarter.

"Tell her to cut us some, too," Frank Sickle said.

"No cook," the woman replied. "Only Squaw Man."

"What the hell does she mean by that?"

"She'll cut a chunk off for you, but you got to cook it yourself," the black man replied.

"Don't we always do our own cookin'?" Clay said.

Little Crow watched the woman carve the meat and hand the chunks to the men. Then, without so much as a glance at each other, the Sickle twins released the rope together and jumped clear. The boom swept upward like a catapult, jerking the rope out from under Strikes the Dog's feet, flipping her to the ground. It hummed through Squaw Man's hands until they clenched tighter, and he rose like a lamb in the talons of an eagle. The counterweight hit the ground, the beef carcass hit the bottom of the timber it hung from, and Squaw Man looked fearfully at the ground as the rope slacked above him. He came down, snapping the rope tight with his weight, and swung six feet above the ground.

The twins laughed, their guffaws sounding like each other's echoes. They slapped their knees alike and stomped rhythm like clog dancers. Strikes the Dog picked up her knife and lunged at them, but Squaw Man dropped in front of her.

"Cook the meat, woman," he said, shoving her toward the tepee. "The boys was just havin' some fun." He looked at the rope burns on his palms.

The squaw's face writhed with anger as she picked up the meat she had dropped and knocked the dirt from it. She stepped over Little Crow on her way back to the tepee, pausing only to kick him once between the shoulders.

As he watched the twins carry their meat toward the cabin, Little Crow heard the squaw rattle a metal bucket behind him at the tepee. His ears trailed the rattling sound to the creek, and he knew she was fetching water to cook with. But the bucket didn't rattle full, and the boy could no longer track the squaw with his ears as she came back. Then the cold wave hit him, and he flinched so hard that his noose choked him.

Strikes the Dog was standing over him with the empty bucket. She rattled it in his face, pointed her finger at him, then at the creek, and shook the bucket at him again. He lay shivering in the mud as she walked back to the creek. Now he knew what she wanted with him. He would be her slave. Carry her wood and water, do whatever else she demanded.

Darkness came and the cook fires flared. Little Crow crawled closer to the iron stake pin, shivering uncontrollably, and began working on the rawhide knot with his teeth.

Eleven

〰〰

He saw the smoke first, then the light of the fires, three miles distant. Claude Duval was sitting on the Medicine Bow Divide, the Snowy Range to his right, a cloud bank far to the west—maybe as far as Utah—glowing like an ocean of floating coals over the setting sun.

Correen's ears had been the first to catch the muffled rumble of gunfire that afternoon, rolling like echoes of distant thunder across the mountain peaks. They had known instantly that Little Crow was in trouble: maybe hiding, maybe captured, maybe killed.

They had spurred their horses to a fast trot and arrived a couple of hours later to find the four dead sheep in the meadow, the dead sheepdog, the great heap of carcasses at the base of the bluff. Claude had ordered the others to stay in camp—Correen against her will—and had taken to the trail after the sheep haters. He had found the boy's moccasin tracks in a few soft places, wincing where Little Crow had left blood on the sharp rocks.

Now it was too dark to read the sign, but it didn't matter. He had spotted their smoke. He climbed to the high seat on Casino's back, the campfires of the Snowy Range Gang in his view. He didn't know what he was going to do when he got there, but he had to have a closer look.

It was pitch-dark when he reached the bluff overlooking the camp. He was on foot, having left Casino a few hundred yards behind. In the firelight he saw the tepee, the unfinished cabin, the meat pole hung with beef. Big gray ghosts were moving beyond camp: the sacred bremmer bulls. Something lay on the ground near the meat pole. Claude thought he saw it move, but he couldn't be sure. A big dog curled up?

He crept silently down the bluff trail, the sound of running water covering his approach. He stopped before crossing the creek, not anxious to get his boots soaked. As he was looking for stepping-stones, or a foot log to cross on, he heard a woman shout from the camp.

"Squaw Man! Squaw Man!"

Boots scuffled on the ground for several seconds, and something thrashed the bushes along the stream above him.

"Wiloughby! The squaw's boy got loose!"

"Goddammit! Come on, boys, let's go find him."

"Tracks go to the creek!"

Claude drew a pistol when he saw the black man approaching with a burning stob, reading the ground. More men appeared up the creek, formless movements in the darkness. One slogged through the water, followed by another. The black man with the torch came closer and Claude thought he would be surrounded, discovered. He shrank into a clump of scrub oak. Three of the outlaws were on his side of the creek now, two still on the side of the camp.

"There he goes!" a new voice shouted—a squeak compared to the black man's baritone.

The brush up the creek popped as if a stampede were coming. Claude saw the boy running, carrying something behind his back: an axe. The black man with the burning stob splashed across the creek to cut the boy's path, crossing right above Claude's hiding place. The boy dropped the axe, but a short man pounced on him from behind. Another man jumped on the pile, orange hair illuminated by the torch.

"Got him!" Wiloughby said.

Claude aimed, but held his fire. The three men were wearing side arms. He would be lucky to get all three in the dark, luckier still to miss the boy. And there were others upstream. He could hear them rustling in the bushes. He wouldn't fire unless they intended to kill Little Crow. He wasn't about to go back to camp and tell Correen he had watched the boy die.

The three men dragged the boy back across the creek, bending his arms up behind him. Claude knew it hurt, but the boy didn't whimper.

"Squaw!" the black man yelled when he had crossed. "We got him!"

Claude heard the ruckus in the bushes upstream again—not the kind of noise an Indian woman would make coming back to camp. Puzzled, he rose from his clump of oak and snuck toward the noise, his Smith & Wesson leading the way.

He couldn't make it out at first: the writhing mass of humanity on the ground. Then he saw a faint glint of red hair, a hand over the squaw's mouth. She was pinned to the ground, but fighting, the man clawing at her clothes. Claude saw her knee hit the redhead in the groin, almost flipping him. The woman squirmed out from under him, stumbled into the creek.

"Shit," the man groaned, humped with pain as he crawled into the darkness upstream.

Claude watched the woman flounder out at the other side of the creek. She ran toward the three men and the captive boy at the meat pole.

Wiloughby was putting a noose around Little Crow's neck. The second redheaded twin, standing there, looked at the approaching squaw, then into the darkness along the creek, a pained expression on his face. He turned quickly toward the cabin, leaving Squaw Man and Wiloughby with the captive.

Were they going to hang him? Claude braced the revolver in both hands for a long shot into camp. No, they were just tying the boy to the sweep. He would have to stand there all night, or his weight would tighten the noose and choke him. Wiloughby picked up a stick from the woodpile and cut the air with it a couple of times.

Now what? Let them beat the boy? He couldn't get them all from this distance with a pistol. The twins were out of sight. He could take Wiloughby out first, but then the black man, if he thought quick enough, would make

Little Crow a hostage—put a gun against his head. Still, he didn't want to see them beat that boy.

Wiloughby was rearing back to hit Little Crow when the Indian woman stumbled up to Squaw Man, grabbing his vest. She made signs with her hands so fast that she seemed to be swatting at mosquitoes, finally pointing back toward the place where the redheaded outlaw had jumped her.

Wiloughby lowered his stick. "What the hell's wrong with her now?"

"Frank! Clay!" Squaw Man bellowed. "Come here!"

Claude saw the twins coming from the cabin together.

"What the hell's goin' on?" Wiloughby demanded.

Little Crow stood shivering, his wet clothes plastered against his skin, the rope tying him close to the timber above his head.

"Which one of you did it?" Squaw Man said as the twins joined the others.

"Did what?" one of them said. They were both wet below the knees from crossing the stream. They wore identical suits, no hats. Each looked as though he had been in a fight.

Squaw Man turned to the woman. "Which one did it?"

She looked at one, then the other, then back at the first. She chose the one to the right and pointed.

"I didn't do nothin' to her," he said.

She pointed at the other, certain now. "Him," she said, jabbing the air in his direction with her finger. "Him, him!"

"I didn't do nothin'," the other twin said.

"All right, both of you!" The black man's rich voice came clearly to Claude across the creek. He walked about halfway to the tepee, then turned around to face the twins, drawing a long knife from a belt scabbard, beckoning the red-heads with the blade.

The twins looked at each other, reached for their knives in tandem, and began flanking the black man.

"Wait just a goddamn minute!" Wiloughby shouted, stalking in between the duelers with his stick. "If I have to sew somebody up, I want daylight. You boys can fight in the mornin'. And, Squaw Man, I don't aim to see my gang killed off now that I just got it back together. If you kill one of 'em, I'll kill you!"

The twins came out of their fighting stances. "What if we git him?" one of them said.

"Oh, hell, you boys don't stand a chance in hell of cuttin' Squaw Man. I don't care if you do read each other's minds, the two of you together ain't half the brawler he is."

"We'll see at dawn," Squaw Man said.

Wiloughby shook his stick at the twins. "You two git back to the cabin. Squaw Man, you git in the lodge. And you . . ." He pointed the stick at the Indian woman. "If that boy gits loose again, I'll bust his skull in."

Claude saw the gang leader wield the stick of firewood viciously overhead, felt his finger tighten on the trigger. But the stick broke across the heavy timber of the meat sweep, above Little Crow's head. The boy flinched, but wasn't touched by the stick.

"You camp right here tonight," the gang

leader ordered, "and make sure he don't get loose again."

The woman got a blanket from the tepee and threw it down beside the boy. She sat there a few seconds, and Claude thought it was all over. But then the woman jumped up and walked to the fire. She pulled out a chunk with a glowing end and came at the boy like a cat stalking game. Little Crow shuddered. Claude felt his muscles tense with dread again, until Squaw Man jumped out of the tepee, took the hot coal away from the woman, and sat her back down on her blanket as he would a child.

Claude watched until the woman rolled herself in the blanket and lay down. It would be a long, cold night for the boy, standing there in the dark. But rescue would come with dawn.

Twelve

❦

Claude found Bob Steck snoring on guard duty, curled up in his blanket with his Winchester. He put his lips next to Steck's ear. "If I'm an outlaw, you're dead," he said.

The old rancher snorted, flinched, and banged himself in the forehead with his rifle barrel. "Hell, Sabinal," he said, his senses restored, "let them others stand guard and I'll make the charge. Did you see the rest of my bremmers?"

"I saw 'em."

"Correen's Indian boy?"

"Yeah. Come on back to camp with me. I don't want to have to tell it but once."

"What about guard duty?"

"No more guard duty tonight. I want everybody to get some rest. You're a worthless guard, anyway, Bob."

When he heard the voices from camp, Claude

held Steck back. "Let's have a listen at what they're sayin' about us before we go in." Claude was still in a mood to reconnoiter. He had always enjoyed sneaking around in the night, whether to line a roost of wild turkeys up against a full moon or to judge his enemy's defenses. And sometimes it made sense to spy on one's own camp.

They snuck close enough to make out the conversation and see the three campers huddled near a small fire. Ike Lafferty was whittling so close to the flames that his shavings flared as they fell. Correen's small hands were wrapped around a tin cup, her hair loose to help keep her neck warm. Claude didn't like her expression. She was smiling at Wolverton as the big man spoke:

". . . so the Pharaoh's men came after 'em, just a-whippin' their horses like stagecoach drivers, except they drove chariots back then. They had six hundred of 'em! Now, Moses' folks were backed up against the Red Sea and somebody said, 'We'd been better off slaves, and now here you've brought us out in the wilderness where Pharaoh can slaughter us.'

"But God used to talk to Moses, just as sure as I'm talkin' to you, and God told him to hold up his walkin' stick and stretch his hand over the sea, and the waters would part. And Moses tried it, and by golly, it worked, and all his folks walked down on the bottom of the sea, and it was dry ground, just like what we're sittin' on. And on either side of 'em, the water rose up like a wall, and they could see fish swimmin' around in there!

"So the only thing that kept the Pharaoh's

chariots and the whole Egyptian cavalry from harassin' Moses' rear was a big ol' whirlwind, or a twister, dark on Pharaoh's side, but bright as fire on Moses' side, so his folks could see their way across the bottom of the Red Sea, because I forgot to tell you that all this happened in the middle of the night.

"Anyway, in the mornin', when Moses had his people across, I guess this pillar of cloud and fire blew away, because Pharaoh took his whole army down onto the bed of the Red Sea after Moses. Now, there was six hundred chariots, and I don't know if they were one-horse or two-horse chariots, but there was a lot of livestock and soldiers down in there.

"Well, all of a sudden, the wheels fell off of all the chariots, and that spooked Pharaoh's men so bad that they called a retreat. About that time, over in Moses' camp, God told Moses to put his hand out over the water again, and when he did, the whole Red Sea slammed back together and you should have heard the hollerin' and screamin' of dyin' men and horses. And in a couple of days all that stock and all those dead soldiers washed up on Moses' side of the sea, and you talk about stink . . ."

Bob Steck burst into laughter. Wolverton and Correen reached for their rifles, but Ike Lafferty merely ceased his whittling and looked into the darkness.

"It's just us," Claude said. "We're comin' in."

Steck was still chuckling when he strode into camp. "Lone Wolf, I'd like to have you tell me the whole Bible that way. I've never heard it explained in the language I savvy."

"I don't understand the half of it myself,"

Wolverton admitted. "It was told by better men than me."

"Any man's better than you," Claude said, muscling his way in between Wolverton and Correen.

Lafferty went back to whittling.

"Did you find Little Crow?" Correen asked.

"I did," Claude answered, soothing her worries with his eyes. "He's alive and well, but tied up and guarded. Looks like the squaw wants him for a slave. I couldn't risk goin' in after him alone, but we'll get him back in the mornin'."

"What's your plan?" Lafferty asked.

Claude squatted by the fire, and the others sat down to hear him. "There's five of 'em. They've got Bob's cattle, so they're the same ones we're all after, no doubt. The leader's name is Wiloughby. He looks like a mean one. The colored feller's called Squaw Man, and he claims the squaw. Then there's the redheaded brothers. Twins. You can't tell 'em apart lookin' at 'em. Their names are Clay and Frank."

"The Sickle twins," Wolverton said. "And Wild Roy Wiloughby. I figured it was them."

Every eye shifted to Wolverton and stared.

"You figured what?" Claude growled.

"They used to come to my Sunday school behind the walls. I confessed all my sins before God and the men in prison. Thought I might get them to do the same, get all them sins off their chests and repent. Wiloughby and the Sickle brothers heard it all: the Creedmoor, the killin', the sign I used to use. I figured it was them that stole Bob's cattle when I heard about the redheaded twins and the leader's pockmarked face."

"You let me go in there without tellin' me who I was up against?" Claude said, glaring at the big man.

"Tried to tell you three times today. You wouldn't listen to me."

"You should've tried harder, damn you."

"I would have if I thought it was that important. Wouldn't have made much difference, though, so I didn't bother."

"You didn't bother? Why, you sorry—"

"Gentlemen!" Correen said. "Can't you put your dashit differences aside until we've rescued Little Crow?"

Claude fumed, but held his tongue. Wolverton looked into the fire like a scolded child. Lafferty seemed to be ignoring them.

"She's right," Steck said. "You two hard cases are gonna have to call a truce if you're gonna be any good to each other or the boy. How do you suggest we go about it, Sabinal?"

Claude heaved, rubbed his face, collected himself. "There's a bluff overlookin' their camp. It's within rifle range."

Steck's eyes shifted as he visualized the elevation. "We'd have to wait for all five of 'em to come out in the open at once."

"There's gonna be a knife fight at dawn."

"What?" Lafferty said, looking up from his whittling stick.

"Those redheaded twins got to foolin' with the colored man's squaw, and he wants to fight 'em both at dawn."

Steck slapped Claude on the back, almost knocking him into the fire. "I told y'all Sabinal was the best. Hell, we'll line up on that bluff like

a firin' squad and perforate every one of the bastards!"

"The squaw is mine," Correen said, brandish-
ing her brass-bellied Winchester. "She'll answer
to me for takin' the lad."

Claude thought it odd to see such a hard set
to the pretty green eyes.

Lafferty nodded. "As long as we stay together
on the bluff, I'm with you. Divide our forces,
and we're beat."

The camp was silent for a moment, except for
the crackling of the small fire.

"You goin' along with all this, Duval?" Wolverton asked, his voice like a bull's moan.

"Why not?"

"Firin' down on people you don't even know?"

"I know they've got Bob's bremmers and
Correen's Indian boy."

"I heard you took your men alive."

"I take rustlers alive if I can. These are kid-
nappers. They've got the boy tied by the neck to
a pole, like a dog. Any one of us misses our
shot, and they'll put a gun to that boy's head,
and then they've got a hostage. No need to risk
it. Shoot 'em all dead—that's the only thing we
can do. Hell, they've left dead bodies from here
to Texas. I'd say they've got it comin'."

Wolverton stood up, lifting his saddle as he
rose.

"Where you goin'?" Claude asked.

"Back to Texas."

The other four exchanged looks.

"You came all the way up here to turn back
now?" Steck said.

"I don't aim to repeat any old mistakes. I

came here to take 'em alive, and if y'all mean to slaughter 'em from ambush, I don't want any part of it."

Correen stood. "We'll be one rifle shy."

"That's not my problem."

She walked toward Wolverton. "Stay and think about it the night," she pleaded. "You may see it our way in the morn."

"No, ma'am. I don't even want to be close enough to hear the gunshots."

"You've lost your nerve," Claude said.

"Think whatever you want. I've learned my lesson. You ought to know better, too, Duval, if Dusty Sanderson was really your friend."

Claude sprang to his feet, jumped across the fire, and lunged at Wolverton. But Lafferty dropped his knife and came between them, moving quicker than Claude ever suspected he might. The rancher caught him by the collar of his jacket and held him back.

"Let him go, Sabinal," he said. "We're better off without him. I wouldn't trust him to hit his man, anyway."

Claude put his hand on Lafferty's forearm and nodded at him. When the rancher turned him loose, he pointed his trigger finger at Wolverton. "I'll catch up to you someday," he said.

Lone Wolf glanced at the men, touched his hat brim for Correen's sake, and disappeared in the dark with his saddle and guns. A minute later, they heard his horse's hooves fade down the trail.

"Better off without him," Claude said. "One less man to watch. I can pick off the two twins, and we'll still rescue the boy. Now, let's rest a few hours."

Bob Steck rolled himself in a blanket. Correen stalked away to her tent. Ike Lafferty picked up his knife and commenced whittling. Claude lay down and watched Lafferty under the brim of the hat he put over his eyes. He was beginning to think of Ike as his surest hand.

Thirteen

◡◦◡

They couldn't see the glow of the rising sun across the mountains, wouldn't feel its warmth for a couple of hours. Dawn came on slowly west of the Snowy Range.

They had left their horses in the trees and crept to the bluff overlooking the outlaw camp. Bob Steck was on the right with his back against a boulder and his rifle on his knee. Correen lay prone in an attitude that Claude found rather distracting. He was next to her, slightly behind her, his rifle propped on the thick branch of a dead pine. To his left, Ike Lafferty stood behind a boulder, ready to hit his mark.

As morning's light came on, Claude made out the shape of the squaw, wrapped in a blanket, still sitting up and guarding the captive boy. Little Crow was shivering, his legs wobbling uncontrollably under him. Every minute or so they would fail him, and the rope would tighten around his neck, then he would have to get his legs under him again.

Correen looked over her shoulder, up at Claude, her eyes holding back tears of anger.

"Wait," Claude whispered.

The features of the camp stood clear in the gray morning light when Squaw Man came out of the tepee wearing his knife in a belt scabbard. "Frank!" he yelled, his echo repeating the challenge three times before it faded. "Clay!" The mountain seemed to tremble at the break of morning calm.

Strikes the Dog didn't even turn to look at her man. She stared at the cabin, waiting for the brothers to appear.

"Oh, hell, Squaw Man," one of them said from the log walls. "We don't want to fight anymore."

"Come out or I'll come in," the black man shouted.

Claude heard Wiloughby's laughter and saw the ugly little cuss come out from the cabin walls. The regulator looked back at Ike Lafferty. Lafferty nodded. Claude looked to his right. Correen and Steck were ready, their thumbs on their rifle hammers. As soon as the knife fight began, they would do it.

He was glad Wolverton had gone. All that damn preaching—and the way Correen listened so contentedly to it—had unsettled him something fierce. He would help Correen rescue her boy while Lone Wolf ran back to Texas.

Strikes the Dog glared at the twins as they passed her, then turned her back to Little Crow to watch Squaw Man fight the Sickle brothers.

The black man drew his long blade, cut circles

with it in the cold air. It would be a tough fight. Squaw Man had seen them act on each other's thoughts before. Still, he was more than a match for them. He would teach them once and for all about fooling with his property.

Claude rubbed the stubble on his chin. He hadn't taken the time to shave before leaving camp, and the growth bothered him. He began easing his Marlin to his shoulder as the squaw got up to get a closer view of the fight. Correen already had her rifle in position, and Bob was settling his on his knees. Then Claude heard Ike's hammer catch over his left shoulder. Lordy, didn't the man know how to cock a rifle silently? He shot a glare toward Lafferty and found the rancher's muzzle staring him in the face.

"Put your hands up, Sabinal," Lafferty said. "You, too, Steck. Both of you get away from your guns. And, Correen, I'll shoot you sure as any man if you try anything. Take your hands off that rifle."

"Ike, what in the hell . . ." Claude whispered, glowering.

"Wiloughby!" the rancher shouted, climbing onto the boulder he had been hiding behind. "Get up here with your guns, you dumb son of a bitch!"

Fourteen

❦

Claude stared up at the muzzle, his heart pounding, his stomach feeling suddenly as cold and heavy as the boulder Lafferty stood on. Of all the stupid things he had ever done . . . He had come to trust Ike Lafferty, a total stranger, after just three nights in camp. Some bit of philosophy Dusty had once uttered came to him: "You can't trust a man till you've got drunk with him."

"Get away from your guns," Lafferty ordered. "Leave 'em there. Move!" He waved his three prisoners away from the rifles left lying on the ground. "Take the gun belt off slow, Duval."

Claude let the twin Russians drop at his ankles and thought about the Le Mat revolver. Still in his saddlebag. Lafferty didn't know about it. Right now he was hoping Correen didn't try anything. She was madder than hell. Probably at herself for the most part. He heard the outlaws scrambling up the bluff on foot.

"Now you, Steck," Lafferty said. "Drop that Colt, and step away from it."

Claude gave Steck a look to calm him. He knew Bob was willing to draw Lafferty's fire, die a hero. But if he did, Claude wouldn't be able to get to Lafferty on top of the boulder quick enough to save himself or Correen. They would have to wait for a better chance, though he didn't see one coming just yet. The Le Mat grapeshot revolver was his only hope.

Steck kicked his Colt away as the outlaws reached the top of the bluff, clouding the air with breath. They stared with open mouths at the three strangers.

"By God!" Wiloughby said, recognizing the old Texan. "You're Bob Steck! How'd you trail me? Who talked?"

Steck stood with his hands clenched, grinding his teeth.

"Frank and Clay, go get our horses," Lafferty ordered, jumping down from the boulder. "In the trees yonder. Squaw Man, you and the squaw cover 'em. Wiloughby, over here."

When Wiloughby got close enough, Lafferty lunged suddenly, bringing his rifle butt around to hit the gang leader in the jaw. The little ruffian managed to block some of the impact with his forearm, but the blow still knocked him down. Lafferty kicked him in the stomach as he got up, then hit him across the back with the rifle barrel.

"Shit, Ike!" Wiloughby squealed. "What's the damn deal?"

"I thought you said you got out of Texas clean!"

"I did, dammit! Somebody must've talked!"

"I thought you said you pinned the cattle rustlin' on Wolverton."

"I damn sure did! I used his sign."

"You didn't do squat, Roy."

The outlaw's eyes shifted to Correen. "Whose little sister is this?"

"She's the widow of that sheepherder I told you to stay clear of until we got rid of the bremmers!" He kicked Wiloughby in the knee, starting him hopping.

"Son of a bitch told me his wife left him!" Roy said, rubbing the joint.

"You expect a man you're about to kill to tell you the truth?"

"Hell, I thought he was too drunk to lie." Wiloughby grinned as he looked Correen over again. "But if I'da knowed she was comin' back, I'da waited."

"You touch her and I'll kill you," Claude said.

Wiloughby smirked. "Who's this longhaired son of a bitch?"

"Name's Sabinal Claude Duval," Lafferty said.

"No bullshit? Away up here in Wyoming? I met a lot of boys you sent to prison, Duval." He frowned at the long locks covering Claude's collar. "This'll make a hell of a scalp for my bridle," he said, reaching.

Claude jerked a fist up into Wiloughby's stomach, snapped a second punch up under his jaw. From the corner of his eye, he saw the squaw moving toward him, but let her take a clean swipe at him with the barrel of the Marlin she had picked up. She caught him on the back of the head, just under the hat brim where no felt would pad the blow. Claude collapsed and braced himself for Wiloughby's boot. He felt the toe jab the tight muscles of his stomach, let the kick flip him, and grunted as if Wild Roy had knocked all the wind out of him.

Correen was over him for a second, then the squaw forced her away.

"Son of a bitch," Wiloughby said, spitting blood down on the regulator.

Claude heard the horses approaching, rolled to all fours, and hung his head as if barely conscious.

"Let's take 'em down to camp," Lafferty said. "Squaw Man, get Duval on his horse."

"We're not gonna kill the girl, are we?" one of the twins asked. "I mean, not yet, anyhow."

"Hell, no," Wiloughby said, grinning. "Not till we get some service out of her."

"If you lay one finger on me, I'll tear you to pieces," Correen said through clenched teeth, her eyes darting frantically.

"Mercy, but don't she talk pretty!" Wiloughby said.

"I said get 'em down to camp!" Lafferty shouted. "We don't have time for you to fool with the woman. We've got to catch Wolverton before he gets off the mountain."

Wild Roy's eyes bulged. "Wolverton? Lone Wolf?"

"Yes, you damn fool," Lafferty was saying. "You had him figured wrong, too. Came all the way from Texas to get you, but didn't like our plans of slaughterin' you all from this bluff. Now you and Frank and Clay are gonna have to go kill him."

Claude stumbled around Casino's hind end as Squaw Man pushed him toward the stirrup. He put his hand on his saddlebag and shot a hidden glance at Steck.

"How come *we* gotta kill him?" one of the Sickle twins asked.

"You brought him here," Lafferty said.

Bob Steck suddenly jumped. He leaped right off the brink of the bluff, into the branches of a lodgepole pine. Claude heard the limbs popping as the rancher fell through them, heard Lafferty shouting orders, felt Squaw Man's rifle muzzle at the back of his head. His right hand, hidden from the black gunman by his body, was unbuckling one of the two leather straps that held down the flap of his saddlebag.

Wiloughby scrambled to the brink of the bluff and shot down at Steck, working his revolver like a pump handle.

Lafferty locked an arm around Correen's neck and put his revolver to her head. "Steck!" he yelled, forcing the woman to the brink. "I've got Correen. You come back, or I'll kill her right now!"

Claude, still acting dazed, shook his head and rubbed the bloody spot under his hat. But his hidden fingers continued unbuckling the saddlebag strap.

"Steck, you hear me?" Lafferty shouted.

"Probably killed hisself jumpin' off," one of the twins said.

"I believe I killed him," Roy said, craning to see over the bluff.

Then the Texan's shaky voice came from below. "Ike?"

"Yeah, Bob."

Like two friends having a conversation.

"Don't hurt her. I ain't goin' nowhere. I think I busted my damn knee."

"See there?" Wiloughby said. "Shot him in the leg."

"Shut up, Roy, and help Squaw Man get Duval on his horse."

Claude hoped no one would notice the strap he had unbuckled as Squaw Man put his foot in the stirrup for him and lifted him into the saddle. He would have to wait to unbuckle the other strap and reach in for the Le Mat.

He held the horn with both hands, swayed side-to-side in the saddle as one of the Sickle twins led him down the trail to camp. The party stopped to lift Steck onto his horse, Steck favoring his right knee, groaning with pain.

Little Crow watched them helplessly as they crossed the creek and went to the pole corral at the edge of the trees. He had recognized Correen on the bluff and felt ashamed that he could do nothing to help her. Now he felt sick with dread for her, because she had come to rescue him. It was his fault. Though the sight of her alive charged his weary legs with energy, he thought about letting his knees buckle, letting his weight tighten the noose around his neck. Watching them abuse her would be a shame he could not bear.

But when Correen got off the horse, she smiled at him and glanced at the longhaired man. Little Crow and Correen could read each other's thoughts almost as well as the evil red-headed twins. Correen's eyes told him there was a chance.

Claude leaned against the saddlebag after

climbing down at the corrals. He put his hat over his right hand and ran his left hand back through his hair, feeling the blood. Under his hat, his fingers groped desperately at the second buckle. Squaw Man's rifle muzzle was against his ribs. Bob Steck was drawing the attention of the outlaws with his busted knee, wailing pitifully as one of the redheads tried to pull him down from the saddle.

"March 'em out there with the boy," Lafferty said.

"Even the girl?" Wiloughby whined.

Steck hopped on his good leg, checked Claude's progress at the saddlebag with a glance.

"Do as I say, or I'll line you up with 'em," Lafferty ordered.

Claude's hand reached into the saddlebag, touched cold Le Mat steel, but then Squaw Man was shoving him away. A loose buckle jingled, but the black man thought nothing of it. Squaw Man marched the regulator into the open, toward the sweep where the boy stood. Steck was limping along behind, guarded by the twins. Strikes the Dog made Correen follow.

"Let's shoot these two," Wiloughby was suggesting, "and take a quick turn or two with the woman before we ride after Wolverton."

Ike shook his head in disgust. "You are no gentleman, Roy. That's what makes you such a damn fool. Don't you understand there's no time for you to defile this girl?"

The Le Mat was getting farther away, hope shrinking.

"I'll make time, dammit." The ugly little rake-hell trotted to the head of the file, drew his Colt, pushed Squaw Man aside. He kicked Claude in the back of the knees, bringing him down. He turned the regulator to face the others, grabbed a handful of long, bloody hair. "Let's get it over with."

The Colt came around toward Claude's face. It was time. He didn't see himself getting out of this alive, but he was not going to go easy on his knees. He would shoot a glance at Correen and Bob, then come alive all over Wild Roy Wiloughby. That had been something, the way Steck had jumped off of that bluff. A good thought to die with. Maybe he could make it to the Le Mat. Probably not.

His eyes flashed at Bob, then Wiloughby's chest exploded. Wild Roy went down as if a rope had jerked him. Claude felt the blood spatter him. The mountain peaks tossed a gunshot among them. A wisp of smoke trailed away from the bluff on a new morning breeze.

Wild Roy Wiloughby had been Lone-Wolfed.

Fifteen

～∞～

It's Wolverton!" Ike Lafferty cried, trying a blind shot at the bluff as he dodged, feeling Lone Wolf's rifle sights on him. The Snowy Range Gang bolted for the trees beside the corral, leaving their prisoners with a few stray shots.

Steck's busted knee suddenly worked well enough to carry him in three great bounds past Claude, to Wiloughby's revolver. The ugly little gang leader was staring at the sky, his body heaving grotesquely.

"Let's go git 'em, Sabinal!" Steck charged the outlaws' rear with a rebel yell punctuated by three shots, chasing them all the way to the cover along the creek. Claude and Correen came to his side at the corrals.

"Give me a knife," Correen said, looking back

at Little Crow, the boy vulnerable to gunshots under the slanting meat pole. "Quickly!"

A bullet hit a corral pole, Ike trying to regroup the outlaws.

Claude ducked under Casino's belly, got the Le Mat and his shaving kit out of the saddlebag. "How many shots you got left?" he asked Steck as he flipped the razor from the groove in its handle.

"Three," Steck said.

Correen was reaching for the razor. He tossed her the Le Mat instead.

"Keep 'em busy." He sprinted for the sweep where the boy was tied, gunshots following him from the trees. He cut the rope above Little Crow's head with a swipe of the razor, pulled the boy behind the bulky counterweight for cover.

Carefully, Claude cut the rawhide binding the boy's wrists. Bullets splintered the long arm of the sweep. He glanced to his right, saw Wiloughby's body, dead. To the left, the sacred bremmer cattle standing in a line, watching the fight with curiosity.

"Ready?" he said, though he wasn't sure the boy understood. He tilted his head toward the corrals and stepped from cover, the boy behind him. He felt a bullet sting the flesh of his inner thigh just before he reached the horses. Bob Steck and Correen were mounting. Correen tossed the Le Mat back to Claude, her hand free to catch the boy's arm and pull him up. Little Crow lit behind her as Claude vaulted into his saddle.

Steck's pistol clicked. He shoved it into his pants and spurred his mount. Claude overtook him, leading the way to the creek. Reaching the water, he plunged in, crossing without drawing fire. At the far side, he turned Casino to guard the others as they crossed, wondering how many rounds the Le Mat had left. He heard the hooves of Wolverton's mount coming down the bluff trail.

Steck was in the middle of the stream, and Correen prepared to plunge in, when Claude saw the squaw racing downstream on the other side of the creek, his Marlin rifle in her hands. "Correen!" he shouted, trying to find a shot at the squaw between the trunks of the oaks and the young lodgepole pines.

A rifle blast from upstream knocked Steck's horse down in the water, pinning the Texan's leg to the streambed. Claude rode by him, spurring Casino back across the creek toward Correen. The rancher's head was above water, the horse shielding him from the gang's bullets. A little cold water wouldn't hurt him.

The squaw raised the Marlin as Correen spotted her and reined toward her, ducking behind the horse's neck for cover. The rifle erupted and Correen's horse collapsed, pitching her and Little Crow into the brush. Claude saw them scramble through the underbrush in different directions. Strikes the Dog charged again as he reached the creek bank. A gunshot cracked and a bullet cut his hat brim. He glimpsed red hair upstream.

The squaw spotted Correen crawling away and stopped to fire, when Little Crow sprang from nowhere, knocking the Cheyenne woman down. As she hit the ground, she fired a round that tore through the boy's ribs, spinning him. Correen screamed.

Claude rode between the two women as the

muffled clatter of hooves came from behind—
Wolverton charging up the creek, attacking the
gang.

Looking down the sights of the Le Mat,
Claude found the squaw on her knees, swinging
the rifle his way, raising the stock to her cheek.
He fired, the .42-caliber load cracking like a
whip after the roar of the big-bore weapons. The
butt of the Marlin splintered in Strikes the Dog's
face, knocking her back as she fired. Claude
pulled the trigger again and heard the click of
the firing pin on a dead shell.

Strikes the Dog sprang to her feet, pumped
the lever of the Marlin, raised the shattered
stock to her cheek, found the longhaired white
man between the tree trunks.

Claude was fumbling with the lever on the
hammer of the Le Mat. He flipped it to fire the
scattergun barrel, raised the weapon, pulled
the trigger as he saw the muzzle of his own
Marlin coming around on him.

Buckshot knocked the Indian woman down.
Wounded, she tried to rise, but Correen was on
top of her, wrenching the Marlin away, using the
last three rifle rounds on her. She dropped the
weapon on the dead squaw and rushed back to
Little Crow.

Claude heard stray shots upstream, the Snowy
Range Gang stampeding away. He rode Casino
through the brush to look down on Correen and
Little Crow. The boy was alive, smiling up at
her, shot bad.

"Oh, laddie," she was saying. "Oh, no . . ."

The regulator reined Casino back to the creek
and found Bob craning his neck to keep his head
above the rapids. "Through with your bath?" he

asked, taking his rope down from the horn strings.

"And ready for a toddy," Steck said, his voice shuddering.

Claude dropped his loop over the saddle horn of Steck's dead horse, took a dally on his own horn, and urged Casino upstream. The big paint searched for footing on the slippery streambed, put his head down, and rolled the carcass from Steck's leg. The rancher got up and staggered in the stream, trying to make his numbed limbs obey.

Claude shook his loop from the dead horse's saddle, grabbed the collar of the rancher's vest, and led him to the creek bank, noticing a limp. "You bust your knee for real this time?"

Steck shook his head. "Just strained it some."

Claude pulled his whiskey flask from his coat pocket, took a swig, and handed it to Steck. He looked upstream to see Wolverton marching one of the redheaded twins back to the camp, both of them on foot. "Where's your horse?"

"Lafferty shot it out from under me. They ran the spare horses off. Left Sickle, here, behind."

Steck shook the whiskey down his throat with a shiver. "Why didn't you kill him?"

"Didn't have to. He was out of shells." He threw Claude's gun belt up to him, the two Smith & Wesson Russians in it. "He was wearin' your guns."

Steck handed the whiskey flask back to Claude, drew the Colt revolver from the front of his pants, and started punching the spent brass casings from it. "Let me borrow some loads," he said to Wolverton.

The big man took six rounds from his belt and

gave them to Steck. Claude broke open one of his Smiths and began reloading with .44s. The captured Sickle brother looked on uneasily.

"Sabinal, let me borrow your horse," Steck said when he had his pistol loaded.

"Where are you goin'?"

"After them rustlers."

"Alone?"

"Just to make sure they ain't doublin' back on us. Come on, get down. A ride will warm me up."

Claude stepped down with his guns and his rope. "All right, but don't go attackin' 'em by yourself. We'd better keep all our shooters healthy if we want to get down from this mountain."

Steck climbed stiffly into the saddle. "Don't do nothin' to that redheaded peckerwood till I get back. I don't want to miss it." He spurred Casino and left at a gallop.

Claude dropped his loop around the outlaw's neck, tightened it, and led him toward the meat pole in the middle of the camp.

Wolverton followed. "What did he mean about us not doin' anything to Sickle?"

"This ain't no time for us to be guardin' prisoners," Claude answered. "Lafferty doesn't mean to let us get off this mountain alive."

Wolverton's eyes shifted nervously. "I won't take part in anything that doesn't sit right with the law or with the Lord."

Claude smirked at the big man. "Don't preach to me, Wolverton. I know what you've taken part in before." He reached the sweep and tossed the end of his rope over it where Little Crow had been tied before.

"How bad is the kid shot?" Lone Wolf asked.

"Bad. Jumped up and took Correen's bullet. Looks plumb proud of himself, dyin' over there." He tied the rope to the timber, taking as much slack out as he could without strangling the outlaw. "I want to know one thing, Wolverton. Why'd you leave last night? How'd you know not to trust Ike?"

"Ike had me fooled," Lone Wolf admitted. "It was you I didn't trust."

"Me?" Claude said, jerking a knot into the rope, looping the loose end around the red-head's wrists.

Lone Wolf nodded. "It was too convenient, you livin' up here so close to Wiloughby's hide-out, leadin' us right to his camp. I figured you were in it with him. I was wrong, of course, and I apologize."

The redheaded outlaw suddenly burst into laughter. "Apologize! My brother's thinkin' about how he's gonna kill you both right now. Damned if he'll apologize."

"Not with his head blowed off," Claude said. He grinned at the worried look on Wolverton's face.

They walked back to the trees to stand over the dying boy. Correen's one hand held Little Crow's while her other stroked the black hair back from his face. He was still smiling, his face pale. Claude saw Wolverton taking off his coat, and quickly unbuttoned his own. They covered the boy with their garments, hoping he would die warm. Claude's coat sleeve fell in a pool of blood when he draped it over the boy, but he let it lie.

They left Correen with Little Crow and stood

speechlessly at the creek for a few minutes, listening, watching the bluffs around them through the treetops. Claude heard a horse galloping and saw Steck returning to the camp. Correen was covering Little Crow's face with Wolverton's coat. They met Steck at the body of the dead boy.

"They hit the high places," Steck said. "I saw 'em go over a ridge, about two miles east." He looked down and saw Little Crow's blood oozing out from under the two coats that covered him. "Sorry about the boy, Correen. I wish I could have taken that bullet for him."

Correen's eyes were wet, alive with anger. She looked each of them in the face, then glared across the open ground, past Wiloughby's body, at the red-haired Sickle twin tied to the sweep.

"What are we gonna do with that Sickle boy?" Lone Wolf said.

"You know fine what we're gonna do," Correen said, her mouth drawn up like an angry child's.

"What?"

Steck adjusted the Colt revolver under his belt. "Hang him from that meat pole, by God."

Sixteen

❧

Clay Sickle saw Steck stalking toward him, favoring a leg. The woman and the long-haired gunman followed. Lone Wolf came along in the rear, uncertainly. But from the looks on the first three faces, the outlaw knew his minutes numbered few.

Steck drew a folding knife from his pocket and cut Claude's rope, leaving a short piece tied around the outlaw's wrists. He untied the long portion of the rope from the timber angling overhead. Keeping the noose tight around Sickle's neck, he led the outlaw to the rope that dangled under the beef carcass at the end of the sweep. He pulled down on the meat rope, but the pole didn't give.

Sickle sniffed.

Correen took hold of the rope, adding her slight heft to the effort. The pole merely bent.

Claude's hands grasped the rope above Correen's, and the three drew their feet up under them, hanging from the meat rope. The counterweight rose an inch from the ground, then settled in its rut again.

"Lend a hand, Lone Wolf," Steck said.

The big man shook his head.

"You wanted part of this manhunt," Claude said. "Now do your share."

"It's justice," Correen added. "He deserves it."

"That's not for us to decide. I refuse to lynch anybody."

Sickle laughed.

"Hell, we don't have to lynch the son of a bitch," Steck said, drawing the Colt from his waist. "I'd just as soon blow his damn head off." He cocked the weapon and put the muzzle against Sickle's greasy red locks.

"Wait!" the outlaw said. "I'll . . . I'll help you. I'll help you pull the meat pole down."

Claude squinted. "Why the hell would you help us hang you?"

Sickle shrugged, searched for words, glanced at the Colt in Steck's hand. "A minute from now just seems like a better time to die."

Steck exchanged looks with Correen and Claude. He put the Colt back into the front of his pants and turned Sickle around to untie his hands. "All right, friend, you've got one last chance to do somethin' good for the world— execute yourself. But try somethin' tricky and I'll gut-shoot you and hang you, anyway." He put the short piece of rope between his teeth.

Sickle rubbed his wrists, paused, stepped up to the meat rope. He saw the eyes of his three executioners guarding him, put his hands with theirs on the rope, pulled with them. The high end of the sweep began to descend. They hauled down on the rope until the beef carcass touched the dirt beside them, and the pole was within reach overhead.

"Stand on the rope," Steck ordered.

Sickle put his boots on the rope and slowly released his grip. The others kept their hold.

"Hands behind your back," Steck said. He held the meat rope with one hand, took the short rope from his mouth with the other hand, and looped it around Sickle's wrist. "Hold this end so I can pull it tight." He pressed a length of rope into the redhead's palm.

The outlaw helped his hangman tie his hands back.

"What's your name?" Steck asked, jerking the knot tight around the doomed man's wrists.

"Frank Sickle." Frank was across the divide somewhere. It was Clay standing next to the beef carcass with the rope around his neck. But Frank was wanted in Nebraska for killing a stagecoach driver and Clay figured his hanging might as well do his brother some good. Frank would know to switch names after today. Hell, he knew already. "He's gonna feel it," Clay said, speaking low.

"Huh?" Claude grunted, catching a strange quiver from the outlaw's shoulder, pressed against his own.

"My brother's gonna feel it when y'all kill me."

Steck scoffed. "Maybe you'll feel it in hell when we kill him." He tied the end of the lynch rope to the meat pole, doubling the knot, pulling it tight. "I'm leavin' you plenty of slack so it'll jerk you up hard. You won't choke slow."

Sickle swallowed, then smirked at Steck. "I'll be obliged to you as long as I live." He chuckled, amused at himself.

"We gonna let go now?" Claude said, anxious to get it over with.

"No," Steck answered, pulling out his pocket-knife again. "I'll cut it." He held the bone handle in his mouth, unfolded a blade with his free hand. "That way nothin' will tangle." He put the blade against the meat rope holding the pole down.

"Don't do it," Wolverton said, his voice a low croak.

Steck looked at the big man over his shoulder. "Hell, Lone Wolf, he's takin' it better than you, and he's the one gettin' hung." His blade sawed through one strand of the lariat; another twisted away.

"Remember, Sickle," Wolverton said, "God forgives."

The third strand stretched and tore. The three executioners fell back as the meat pole whipped upward, cutting the air with a sigh, moaning on its fulcrum, carrying the beef carcass with it. Clay Sickle suddenly took an urge to run, thinking maybe the lynch rope wouldn't jerk him quite so hard if he got out from under the pole. He had taken three steps when his slack played out—a short whir of the tightening noose, a thump of tension, a groan of stretching fibers.

Sickle's legs kicked once, froglike, as his boots left the dirt. The body rose like a rocket, tracing a curve in the air as the rope swung it back to center.

The counterweight hit hard and bounced, the high end of the long timber springing like the tip of a cane pole, the beef carcass hitting its underside. The lynch rope slacked, the body arching high through the air, as if shot from a cannon. It reached a zenith, then fell like a goose killed on the wing, limp, plunging headfirst toward the ground.

The rope was going to tighten and whip the dead man around like a calf hitting the end of a lariat. Claude doubted a human neck could take it, and he turned away. He found himself looking into Wolverton's damning stare as he heard the lynch rope snap taut and creak against the meat pole.

His eyes escaped Lone Wolf's glare and found Correen staring toward the corpse, her face suddenly pale, her mouth open. Then the body swung between them, its neck bent like an elbow, the dead man's eyes looking through Claude, like Wolverton's, damning him.

"Son of a bitch!" Steck cried. "I didn't think it would hang him that hard. It's a wonder his damn head didn't come off!"

As they watched the body swing, an echo reached the valley: maybe the caw of a crow or the morning bark of a stray coyote. Or maybe, Claude thought, the yell of a redheaded outlaw feeling the lynch rope tighten around his brother's neck.

Seventeen

❧

Amen," Wolverton said, putting his hat back on his head. He got down on his knees and pushed the first handful of dirt in on Little Crow's body, wrapped in a blanket in a shallow grave.

Claude put his hand on Correen's shoulder for a moment, then began pushing dirt in with his boot.

"What do we do next, Sabinal?" Steck said.

Claude thought about Ike Lafferty, Squaw Man, the other Sickle twin. "We'll ransack this camp for anything we can use. Lafferty will do the same to our camp over the divide. We've got one horse. Can't chase 'em down and attack. Can't even run."

"They'll come back after us," Steck said.

Claude nodded. "Probably not today. We've got one more gun than they do, and we've got 'em scared. They know we're short on ridin' stock and can't get out of the mountains anytime soon, so they'll probably go back to Ike's ranch and get some more boys."

"Yes," Correen said, throwing handfuls of dirt onto the blanket. "Lafferty will come back after us with twice as many men."

"We'll get ready for 'em," Claude said, nodding to convince himself. "The bastards will think they've never seen a fight before."

"That's what I like to hear!" Steck brandished a fist.

Lone Wolf looked up from the graveside. "Now we're the Snowy Range Gang, and they're the posse. 'Whatsoever a man soweth, that shall he also reap.' "

Claude groaned. "Bob, go up on the bluff and stand guard," he ordered.

Steck didn't care much for guard duty, but grave digging appealed to him even less. He picked up his rifle and limped away from the fresh grave. By the time he was in place on the bluff, Claude had put the last stone on the mound. He left Correen and Wolverton and went to find his Marlin rifle.

The weapon was still lying across the body of Strikes the Dog, where Correen had dropped it. The bullet from the Le Mat had splintered the stock, the hardwood cracked from grip to butt as if by an axe. Only a few grains held it together.

Claude went back to the tepee and found a square of rawhide. He cut a spiral from it, making a narrow strip about six feet long. He put the rawhide strip under a rock in the creek to soak, also rinsing Little Crow's blood from the sleeve of his coat.

When he came back to camp, he saw Wolverton dragging Roy Wiloughby's body to the meat pole. The big man cut the Sickle brother down, then dragged both dead men to a shallow grave he had dug.

Claude shook his head. He would have left the outlaws to the buzzards. At least Lone Wolf had the decency not to bury them near Little Crow. They were across the camp from the Indian boy, Little Crow on higher ground.

Claude found Correen working at the tepee, making herself useful, putting the contents of the lodge into two piles. One was made up of usable things: blankets, food, guns. The other pile was for things of no value: skins, holey buffalo robes, trinkets.

Claude picked up Squaw Man's .45-70 Winchester. "Find any ammunition for this thing?" he asked, looking up at the bluff to make sure Bob Steck was still on guard, and not off engaging the enemy.

"Maybe fifty rounds," she answered. Much of the pleasant lilt had left her voice this morning.

Claude grunted, saw Wolverton coming. "There'll probably be more in the cabin."

"Why was he smiling so?" she said quietly, looking at a piece of tanned deerskin, as if unaware that the thought had escaped. "Didn't he know he was dying?"

Claude rubbed his chin and wondered where he had dropped his razor. "Proud of himself. He wanted to do right by you because you came to rescue him. Gave him a chance to die a hero. He did all right."

Correen saw through Claude and what he was

trying to do: ease her guilt. She gave him a forced smile for trying.

Wolverton strode up to the pile of goods Correen had tossed aside from the tepee. "Mind if I have this?" he said, picking up an old buffalo robe.

"What on earth would you want with it?"

"I'm gonna wrap the Indian woman in it."

Correen looked at Claude, then back at Wolverton. "Whatever for?" she said.

"Bury her."

She threw an old saddle blanket into a pile and scowled at Wolverton. "Leave her to the wolves!"

Wolverton picked up the robe. " 'Rejoice not over thy greatest enemy being dead, but remember that we die all.' "

"Do not quote the Good Book to me, Mr. Wolverton. I rejoice in nothing this morning!" She threw the bearskin flap aside from the entrance hole and stepped into the tepee.

Claude caught a part of the anger she left behind. "How the hell can you leave a good man to burn in his own fire, then bury a bunch of dirty outlaws?"

Wolverton winced. He had been wondering when Duval would remind him of Dusty Sanderson again. "Too late to take back the things I've done. All I can do is change."

Claude faked a laugh, then stepped closer to Wolverton, glaring. "I hope you don't think I'm gonna let you go back to Texas alive just because you saved my life this mornin'." He stalked away toward the creek.

The strip of rawhide he had put in the creek was soft now. He pulled it between his fingers to wring some of the water from it, then began wrapping it carefully around the split stock of his Marlin. He tucked the end under the last three coils, fiddled with it until it was snug.

The sun was shining down on the outlaw camp now, so Claude carried his rawhide-wound Marlin out into the light. He propped it against the counterweight of the meat sweep at such an angle as to catch the hottest rays of the sun.

As his eyes swept upward to check on Steck's position, he caught an unexpected movement about halfway up a tree. It was Wolverton, putting the squaw to rest the Cheyenne way, on a platform of poles built into a tree. He shook his head in bewilderment.

Correen stopped at the meat pole on her way to search the unfinished cabin. "I don't know what to think of him," she said, watching Wolverton hoist the shrouded body into the tree. He's either a better Christian than I or a dashit fool."

"I don't believe he's either one of those."

"Why don't you use one of the Winchesters?" she asked, observing his rawhide-wrapped rifle stock in the sunshine.

"I've grown partial to that Marlin."

"Why? Certainly it shoots no better than a good Winchester."

"Winchester's a good gun, but when you have to shoot fast, it goes to slingin' those spent shells over your head, up under your hat brim. That side-eject puts the Marlin one up in my judgment."

She shook her head. "You with your twin pistols and your fast-shootin' repeaters. You're a short-trigger man, Mr. Duval."

"Come on. Let's have a look in that cabin."

Stepping through the doorway sawed into the new log wall, Claude found wads of blankets and clothes, stacks of dirty pots and pans, coils of ropes and piles of tools. A rifle leaning against the rear wall caught his eye, its long barrel sticking through a hole cut in the end of a leather saddle scabbard.

"Look here," Claude said, stepping across the cabin to the weapon. "I'll wager the caliber of that piece is .44-90." As he pulled the rifle from the scabbard, a checkered pistol grip appeared. Then a long-range tang sight, folded down. Then the single-shot falling-block action, about three feet of octagonal barrel, and a hooded front sight. Claude had never before held such a piece. He had seen only one, in the courtroom during Wolverton's hearing.

"Sharps Model 73 Creedmoor," he muttered. "The same kind of gun Wolverton used to kill with."

"I've seen a Creedmoor rifle before," Correen said. "I'm sure it was a Remington, and not a Sharps."

Claude shouldered the weapon, its barrel longer than a goose gun's. "Remington's made some. So has Ballard, and Wesson, and some others. Sharps still makes one, too, but they use .45 caliber now. The old 73 model was the only Sharps Creedmoor to chamber a .44."

Correen held her hand out for the weapon, tested its balance when Claude handed it to her. "Mr. Creedmoor had a lot of partners," she said, putting the slender stock to her cheek.

Claude chuckled. "Creedmoor's not a fellow's name. It's the name of a shootin' range at Long Island, New York. They have long-range matches there." He took the rifle back from her. "Creedmoor's just another name for a long-range gun." He showed her the hooded sight on the barrel tip. "The front sight's got a level in it, and you can adjust it for windage." He flipped the rear tang sight up. "And you can adjust this one to a thousandth of an inch for distance."

"How far will it shoot?"

"They use 'em up to a thousand yards in match shootin'. Now, you take an expert like Wolverton. If he lays down on his stomach and judges wind and distance right, he might kill a man a thousand yards away. He got Wiloughby this mornin' at about two hundred yards with a regular Winchester. Four or five hundred yards is a sure thing for him with a good Creedmoor rifle."

Her cold eyes studied him. "You sound as if you admire him for it."

"I admire marksmanship. Like you shootin' that brass casing out of the air. But I cannot abide a murderer."

A shadow filled the doorway, and Lone Wolf stepped in, quickly sensing the eyes on him. He stopped, saw the rifle in Duval's hands.

"I found you somethin' to work with," Claude said, pitching the Creedmoor across the cabin.

The big man had to catch the gun, his left hand grasping the forestock, his right the checkered grip. He turned the weapon a couple of times, letting the sun glint from its facets. He let it lie upside down in his open palms. One side of his mouth smiled, but only for a second, then his eyes bulged as if entranced by the evil stare of a rattlesnake he held in his hands.

"Remember how to use it?" the regulator asked. He saw Wolverton flinch and found the Creedmoor flying back at him.

Lone Wolf stumbled back out of the cabin, wiping his palms on his shirt. He tripped over the threshold and fell backward into the sunlight. He rolled and ran, like a scared child.

Claude stepped to the doorway with the rifle in his hands, Correen coming up beside him. They watched the big man stumble forward into the brush along the creek.

"My God," Correen said. "What got into him?"

Claude stood silent for a second, watching the place where Wolverton had disappeared. He held the Creedmoor before him one-handed like a flagstaff. "The devil, I reckon."

Eighteen

❧

Frank Sickle sat on his horse, his head cocked at an unnatural angle, watching Ike Lafferty and Squaw Man as they pulled up Correen's bow tent and threw it into the fire.

"Get off your horse, Frank, and lend a hand," Lafferty said.

"I'm Clay."

Lafferty squinted. Usually, neither brother complained when called by the other's name. No one could tell them apart, anyway. "I thought that was Frank's horse."

"They hung Frank," Sickle said.

"I wouldn't doubt it." Lafferty added a pack saddle to the blaze. "Old Steck's been itchin' to kill somebody."

"What about my woman?" Squaw Man asked, as if Sickle could conjure a vision of her.

"I hope they hung her, too," the redhead said.

Squaw Man's mouth pulled tight across his teeth. He reached for his reins and bounded into the saddle.

"Hey, where you goin'?" Lafferty demanded.

"Goin' back to see about the squaw."

"Don't be a damned fool. They're not in the frame of mind to take prisoners. Like Frank says, they probably hung 'em if they didn't shoot 'em."

"I'm Clay," Sickle repeated. He scratched at his neck, starting at the throat, working all the way around to the back. His skin was red from clawing. It had started itching right after he had caught the crick in his neck. He had been riding at the time, crossing the divide, and the pain had struck him like a knife between his neck joints. He had coughed, and wheezed, and almost fallen out of the saddle.

Squaw Man held a tight rein. "What are we gonna do?"

"Use our heads. They've got one more gun than we do now, and believe me, that sheep woman can shoot as good as any of us. On top of that, they've got the Creedmoor. Wolverton can kill a man at five hundred yards with that thing, so we don't want to just go chargin' in after 'em."

"We ain't lettin' 'em go," Squaw Man insisted.

"They aren't goin' anywhere," Lafferty replied. "They've only got one horse left. Frank shot Steck's horse down in the creek. The squaw shot that horse out from under Correen and the boy. When we turned to run, I fired over my shoulder and killed Wolverton's horse, and we drove all the spare mounts off with us. Duval is the only one left with a mount."

"So what?" Sickle said.

"They can't all four ride one horse. The worst they could do is send somebody out for help. That's why you two are gonna go back and watch 'em from a distance. If one of 'em rides that big paint horse out of camp, you hunt 'im down. I'll go back to the ranch, round up some of the boys, and be back in a couple of days. Then we'll finish 'em off."

"Then what?" Squaw Man said. "What about the bremmer cattle? The gang?"

"You'll scatter the bremmers. Trade 'em to the west. If anybody comes up from Texas lookin' for Steck, I'll tell 'em the Snowy Range Gang killed him and got away with all his cattle. Then you'll build up another gang, Squaw Man, and come next spring, it'll be business as usual. Hell, it's a blessing to get shed of Wild Roy. He'd of got us all caught sooner or later."

Sickle was rubbing his neck. He felt a chill. Looking to the east, he saw clouds building. He found breathing difficult—pressure on his chest. "Let's go," he said, buttoning his coat up to the collar. "I don't feel worth shit."

Nineteen

Damn, I hate this," Steck said. He was helping Claude and Correen raise the lodge poles near the base of the Snowy Range.

"It'll keep your rear end out of the weather," Claude said, glancing at the darkening sky.

"I don't mean the tepee. I mean sittin' up here waitin' to get shot at."

They had made a travois of the lodge poles, using Casino to haul everything of value five miles up from the outlaw camp. Now the Snowy Range loomed above them, a colossal wall of rock jutting above the timber, marked with streaks of snow. Several high mountain lakes nestled between the Snowy Range and the trees, huge pools of ink today, drawing darkness from the storm clouds that had gathered overhead. Claude had chosen to camp beside a body that

Steck had named Lake Correen—Loch Correen, as her mouth spoke it.

"The fishin' rod was for Little Crow," she had said, looking out over the clear pool. "If only he had lived to use it."

Wolverton was somewhere in the timber. He hadn't spoken to anyone since running from the Creedmoor. He had come back to camp, his eyes as red as if he had been on a three-day drunk, but he hadn't spoken a word.

"We don't have a choice," Claude said. "We have to fort up and wait. Might as well count our advantages and quit whinin' about our sorry luck."

"What advantages?" Steck said, using a big rock to pound an iron pin into the ground near the center of the lodge. A rawhide strap running from the pin to the crossed tops of the lodge poles would hold the tepee firmly to the ground in case the wind got up.

"Well, we can pick our own ground," Claude said.

"That's true. I want to die over there," Steck said, pointing. "How 'bout you, Correen?"

Correen's dark laughter felt good, but didn't last long.

"We've got the Creedmoor. Wolverton can hold them off at five hundred yards or better with that."

"No." The voice croaked from the tree line. Wolverton followed it to the campsite and began unfolding the old hides that would cover the lodge poles. "I won't use that Sharps or any other gun against any man, except to defend myself or one of you." His eyes were clear now, bright and sure.

"That's what I'm talkin' about," Claude said. "Shoot 'em before they can get in range of us."

Wolverton shook his head. "I won't fire unless they fire at us first."

"The hell you won't!" Claude shouted, his voice hitting the rocks and bouncing back. "If they figure out you're not gonna hold 'em back, they'll move in range and rush us."

Wolverton shook his head. "I can't. The Good Lord's testin' me."

Claude's mouth dropped open, and he stared at the old killer.

"There goes another advantage." Steck groaned, but he was actually enjoying this. The worse it got, the more he liked it. "That Creedmoor might as well be just another gun with any of us lookin' through the sights." He helped Correen and Wolverton spread the hides around the framework of lodge poles. It blocked the cold wind and mist, made him eager to get a fire going.

Claude stood and stared at Lone Wolf in disbelief while the others worked. He put his hands on his hips, noticed his breath trailing away on the cold wind. It was summer down in Texas, green grass sprouting from Dusty's grave on the plains. But up here it was freezing cold. Raindrops began to thump against his hat brim.

Steck built a fire in the tepee, and Correen began cooking. Claude carried in the guns. Wolverton brought in everything else. They sat in a circle in the captured hide tent, staring at the spaces between one another. Wolverton's eyes avoided looking at the Creedmoor, standing tall where it leaned against a lodge pole.

Claude went out, filled a small pot with lake

water, put it over some coals, and found his shaving kit. He sat down again to think and wait for the water to heat up.

"There's ranches down in North Park," Wolverton said, breaking the silence. "Correen could ride the horse down and bring back help."

"You'd all be dead by the time I got back," she said quickly.

"*If* you got back," Claude added. "Ike may have left Squaw Man and that other Sickle boy behind to watch us. One rider's too easy to ambush." He smirked. "Anyway, if anybody was to try it, it would be you, Wolverton. Correen's too valuable to us. She's willin' to fight."

They stared at the lodge poles again, the tension between them like a snowbank.

"Correen, how many rounds did we find for the Creedmoor?" Claude said after a minute.

"No more than twenty, if that many."

Claude spread the contents of his shaving kit on a rag in front of him. "Wolverton, you're gonna teach me how to shoot that damn long-range Sharps. We've got a couple of days to practice before Ike comes back with his boys."

The big man shook his head. "You'd use all your rounds and still not be worth a darn."

"Then we'll reload the damn cartridges! Take some powder from some other shells!"

"We don't have primers or bullet molds," Correen said, glancing up from the fire.

"Anyway, what's the difference in my shootin' 'em or teachin' you to?" Wolverton said. "I won't have part of it either way."

They fell silent again, listening to the bacon sizzle, smelling the aroma. Claude got up once to put his finger in the water, then sat back down.

"All right, how's this?" he said, turning to Wolverton. "We'll find an open place where we can see five hundred yards or so. When Ike and his boys find us, I'll ride out on Casino and draw their fire. If they shoot at me, you'll have to shoot back, right?"

"Better to let me draw their fire," Correen said, turning the bacon in a skillet. "I'm smaller and lighter. I can ride faster and will make a smaller target."

"Now, wait just a doggone minute," Steck said. "I ain't no braggart, Correen, but I can out-ride you. And you're a better rifle shot than me, so we'd be better off lettin' me draw their fire while you and Sabinal and Lone Wolf cover me."

"Stupid plan," Wolverton said. "They'll shoot our only horse out from under you, then we'll be in a worse fix."

"Don't talk to me about stupid!" Claude shouted. "You're the one too damn stupid to shoot for your own life! The only chance we've got is to whittle their forces down with that Creedmoor before they get inside of normal rifle range!"

Wolverton's dark face frowned, but he said nothing.

Claude dipped his shaving brush in the hot water and began viciously whipping up soap. "Where's the best place to fort up, Correen?"

She pulled her dark hair back and bent over the fire again, crouching, balancing on her toes with the agility of a bird. "If we're lookin' for open ground to fight on, I would say to go to

the south, along the divide where the wind
gnarls the trees so." She paused, stirred the
beans. "I wish Little Crow was here. He knew
every canyon. He grazed sheep on the western
slope, shot deer to the south, hunted mustangs
north of the Snowy Range. He could tell us
where to hide an army."

Claude's shaving brush pulled slowly away
from his face, leaving a smear of white soap. He
looked at Correen, found her stirring beans.
He looked at Steck, found him pouting across
the tepee. Then he looked at Wolverton and
found the big man looking back, eyes ablaze
with new energy.

"Mustangs?" Claude said.

Correen looked up from the fire. "Yes, a small
band of them north of here."

"Why didn't you say so before?" He rinsed
his brush in the hot water, yanked the rag out
from under his shaving tools, and wiped the
soap from his face.

"Why would I mention it?"

"Horses, Correen! With mounts we can take
the fight to Lafferty!"

She gawked. "But these are wild horses."

"I've rode green stock before."

"It's not possible," Correen argued. "These
horses have never worn a saddle."

"I broke horses with the Indians when I was a
boy," Wolverton said. "I can train 'em good
enough to ride in three days. Maybe even two."

"How you gonna catch 'em?" Steck said.
"Might be able to rope one or two if Sabinal's
big paint can get close enough."

Correen pulled a skillet from the fire. "Little
Crow said he built a trap across the mouth of a

canyon. A high fence of poles and brush. I brought him some salt and an auger so he could make a salt lick to attract them."

"How long ago was this?" Claude asked.

"Weeks. He said he would give them time to get used to the pen, then sneak back and catch them in it, close the opening with some poles he had cut and left there."

Claude wrung his hands together, put his razor back in the shaving kit. "Where is this trap?"

"North of the Snowy Range and east of Rock Creek. That's all I know."

"That's enough." He stood up and put his coat on.

"Where are you going?"

"Saddle up Casino. I'll eat some supper, wait for dark, then slip out of camp. Head north. With some luck maybe I can find the boy's mustang trap in the mornin' and catch us some horses."

As he left the tepee, he rubbed the coarse stubble on his chin, almost glad now that he hadn't found time to shave. A little whisker would keep his face warm tonight in the freezing rain.

Twenty

❧❦❧

The boy had built a damn fine trap. Claude looked down on it from the bluff, his stomach growling against the rimrock, the warm morning sun drying his backside. It seemed he was getting to know Little Crow better now, and was liking him.

He quietly raked some gravel out from under his belly and settled in again, like a rattler taking sun on the rocks. He was more comfortable than he had been all night.

After leaving the tepee, he had ridden east around the Snowy Range, then loped north for an hour in the sleet, until it became too dark to see. He had dismounted, rolled himself in a blanket, a tarpaulin folded below and over him. No fire. Little sleep.

It had snowed briefly before the clouds broke, about midnight, letting the moonlight through.

He had mounted again and continued north, riding at a walk, listening to the wolves howl and the panthers scream, knowing the mustangs heard them, too. He found Rock Creek, made another camp, caught an hour of sleep before sunrise.

He was riding Casino in the creek when he found the crossing. The mustangs had used the ford often, their unshod hooves stomping down the brink of the creek bank. Their trail seemed to lead toward a narrow canyon to the east.

He rode wide around the downwind side, peered into the canyon from the rim above. Now, from the bluff, where the sun thawed him out, Claude studied the barricade built across a narrow place in the canyon floor. Little Crow had strapped stout poles to pine saplings with rawhide. He had laced the pole fence with brush and evergreen boughs, copper-colored now, making the barricade appear solid up to seven feet high. He had left an opening in the middle, through which the mustang trail led. Claude could see the cut poles lying ready to close the gap, a pile of pine boughs and brush nearby.

The sun was making him drowsy, but he fought off sleep. Mustangs might come and go before he knew it. He hoped they'd want to gnaw at Little Crow's salt lick today. Tomorrow might be too late. He put his palm on the rocks, rested his chin on the back of his hand, waited.

The others would be well on their way by now, carrying guns, saddles, and provisions on their backs. He hoped they wouldn't get here too soon and spook the mustangs. Not likely, though. A long walk. He'd have to go back and find them. First, catch the mustangs. Then find

the others ... Yes, find them ... Find Correen ... Correen ...

A clatter woke him, and he felt a chill. The rimrock was in the shade now, the sun behind a tree.
Must have been asleep an hour, he thought. What
about the mustangs? What was that sound?

His eyes focused on horses below, moving like
deer among islands of brush. His heart pounded
against the rock. A dream? He saw the stallion
lunge, nipping at a mare's flank, chasing her
back into the band, hooves rattling like an alarm
clock. They were real. The steel-gray stallion,
four mares, and a foal.

They approached the barricade cautiously,
nostrils flaring, ears pivoting, necks craning.
Only the foal took time to gambol, rearing back
from a windblown blade of grass, kicking his
heels. The lead mare stepped inside the barricade and stood, head high, for almost a minute.
Then she lowered her nose and stalked toward a
log on the ground.

Claude hadn't noticed before, but the log had
been bored with holes and gnawed into a rough
hourglass shape. The holes, once filled with salt,
were now empty. The lead mare sniffed the log,
moved farther up the canyon. The stallion
herded his other harem members into the trap as
the lead mare nuzzled another log, also with
holes bored in it.

Little Crow had set his baits perfectly. Now
the lead mare was checking the third salt lick,
also empty. She continued searching for a fresh
lick, taking the herd all the way around a bend
in the canyon.

The stallion, bringing up the rear, stopped and

turned to look once at the hole in the barricade. He waited long enough to let the lead mare get to the head of the canyon. If anything was wrong, she would scream and come galloping out. But she did not. The old boy tasted salt. He waited a few more moments, then walked up the canyon, around the bend.

Carefully, Claude slid back from the rim of the canyon and pushed himself to his knees. He was stiff from sleeping on the rocks but determined to control his every movement. One clattering rock or breaking branch would warn the wild horses, and his slim hopes of obtaining mounts would vanish.

He used several minutes getting into the next canyon, where he had left Casino, all the while imagining the mustangs trotting out of the trap and escaping across the valley. He finally mounted, made Casino walk. He didn't want hooves warning the mustangs. It wasn't easy, for he wanted to get there before the wild horses left, but he remained calm and walked.

Rounding the bend to Little Crow's canyon, Claude saw no sign of the wild horses. Either they were still up in the head of the canyon or they had left. He rode quietly toward the narrow place where the boy had built the barricade. A hundred yards from the gate, he saw the lead mare appear around the bend. She flinched as if stung by a hornet, whistled, and lunged back toward the head of the canyon.

Claude put spurs to Casino, and a thunder of hooves shook the canyon. He had a good idea what would happen. The mustangs would charge to the head of the canyon, see that they were trapped, and stampede back toward the opening in the barricade. He would have to get it closed before they returned, otherwise he might not be able to turn them.

As he hit the ground beside the gap, he could hear the stallion screaming at his mares. He grabbed a pole that Little Crow had left, and slid it into its notches, starting with the top rail. By the time he had the second pole in his hands, the percussion of hooves had burst around the bend in the canyon, and the horses were galloping his way.

He tried not to look up as he put the second rail in place, but he caught a glimpse of the huge gray stallion charging, neck bowed, ears back, legs sprawled. He got the rail in its notches and looked again. The mares and the foal had dropped back, but the stallion was challenging. Claude took off his hat and waved it, whistled, hollered, and jumped up on the lower rail so he would stand taller.

Casino began grunting and pulling against the bridle reins as the gray beast came on. He felt an old twinge of wild savagery but restrained himself, too long under the saddle.

The gray finally planted his hooves just a few leaps short of the gate. He stood whistling breath from his nostrils, glaring with defiance, too proud to turn tail. He reared and slung his head as he backed away. Finally, he wheeled, kicked toward Claude, and darted after his mares, pawing them, biting, driving them up the canyon.

Claude wrapped Casino's reins around a branch, hoping the big paint wouldn't pull loose to fight the gray. He put two more rails in place. If he hadn't known better, he might have thought there was an avalanche coming down from the head of the canyon.

The gray stallion stopped even closer this time as Claude stood in front of Casino, waved his hat, and hollered. He didn't want to give away his location to Squaw Man or the Sickle twin by shooting, but he was ready to reach for a Smith & Wesson if the gray decided to do more than bluff. He couldn't afford to get Casino hurt in a fight. But the big gray turned tail again and angled across the canyon floor, looking for a trail out of the trap.

Claude began lacing brush into the new section of fence. He spaced the dried pine boughs out at first, then started filling in the gaps between them as the wild herd thundered down the canyon a third time.

The regulator leaped into the saddle, felt Casino trembling under him. He stood in the stirrups and waved his hat high, shouting at the stallion across the barricade. The big gray was fuming now, grunting, slinging his head in rage. He stopped just short of the fence, reared and pawed at Casino through the brush. His hooves came down on the rails as a screaming roar rattled from his lungs in a cloud of vapor.

Claude was holding a tight rein on Casino, but the big paint was feeling his mustang blood.

The gray dropped behind the brush barricade for a second, then reappeared, wall-eyed, ears low, lips curling back from his teeth. He pawed blindly, parting brush, and came across the top rail, his belly bowing the stout pine pole.

"Oh, dammit!" Claude yelled, wrapping a hand around his right-hand revolver.

The gray wielded his head like a battle axe and

climbed the fence rails with his hind hooves. He stumbled as he cleared the barricade, landing on his knees, using his face to break his fall.

Claude spurred Casino between the wild stud and the hole he had started in the fence. The gray came up off his knees and bit Casino on the shoulder. The paint roared with rage and sprang forward, bumping the gray, then felt the bit in his mouth and gave ground, guarding the opening in the fence.

The gray reared and pawed, hopping toward the horse and rider on his hind legs. Claude drew his pistol. Casino wanted to rear and face the attack but remembered his training and stayed on all fours, letting the gray come down on him.

Claude was swinging the barrel of his .44 up when the huge mass of gray landed in his lap and bounced, the stud thrashing head and hooves everywhere. The hot gray horse was on his hand, his revolver, his reins. He had no control over Casino now, astounded that the paint hadn't collapsed under the weight.

He reached for his left-hand pistol as Casino whirled right, dropping his head. The gray flinched, screamed, and Claude knew his mount must have sunk teeth into a thigh. The wild stud slipped down over Casino's neck, throwing hooves like a prize fighter as he retreated. One chopped the back of the rider's hand against the saddle horn.

The gray stumbled back and gathered himself for another lunge when Claude jerked his trigger. The four mares and the foal shied away across the barricade and thundered up the canyon. The gray darted aside, lowered his neck, and ran, abandoning his harem in the trap, his instinct for survival overcoming his love of combat. His huge gray rump shrank away toward the creek. Then he was gone, his screeching roar sounding across the valley, drowning out the echo of his hooves.

Claude stumbled down from the saddle, holstered both revolvers, and had a look at Casino. The paint's muzzle was red, but that was the gray's blood. A couple of bites on the shoulders, a cut or two on the neck. Nothing too deep. He stepped in front of the stallion and saw Casino's ears angle back.

He popped the paint across the muzzle and held his head down with the reins. "Don't you cock your ears at me!" he said, not interested in getting bitten. He stared the stallion down until Casino shook his head, pitched his ears forward, and heaved.

Claude grinned. "I know you could have whipped him, but I can't have you all cut up." He reached out to pat the paint's broad neck and saw something flapping on the back of his right hand. A hunk of skin, peeled back by the gray's sharp hooves. He stared, as if at someone else's wound.

"Oh, shit," he muttered, remembering the blow from the hoof on the saddle horn. He had felt a little pain, but expected only a scratch. Now it hurt like hell, of course. And no time to fool with it. The mares were coming back.

He pressed the skin down on the back of his hand, avoided looking at it, and started repairing the damage the big gray stallion had done to the barricade.

Twenty-one

Correen saw plainly where the tracks were leading, but she kept quiet and let Wolverton go ahead of her to read the sign.

The big man paced, searched the ground, then stopped. "I figured he might ride into the creek sooner or later," he said, lowering his saddle to the gravel. "Doesn't want the mustangs to smell him on the ground."

Correen dropped her saddle. Across it, she put a Winchester and the Creedmoor, which Wolverton had refused to take up. "Shall we camp here until he comes back for us? We don't want to stumble onto Little Crow's trap and frighten the wild horses away." Her joints were aching from the hike, her arm and shoulder muscles burning from carrying the load.

Steck dropped his tack beside Correen's. "Ain't no easy way to carry a saddle if you ain't a horse." He had woken this morning to find his right knee swollen tight inside his pants leg where his horse had fallen on it the day before. He had walked in the rear all this morning, so the others wouldn't see him limping. "I ain't marched so damn much since the war. Hated it then, too."

Correen began gathering wood for a cook fire. Claude would be hungry when he came back.

"I'm gonna have a look around," Wolverton said. He stood over Correen's saddle for a moment, staring down on the weapons. She saw his eyes on the old Sharps, the fear still in them. He reached toward the gun but grabbed a Winchester instead, and left.

Steck rolled himself in a blanket and put his hat over his face.

Correen stacked her kindling, took in a deep breath of cool mountain air. This was a pleasant place, the sun shining down through the leaves of small oaks, Rock Creek rushing nearby. If only they had rescued Little Crow. How different she might feel now. And yet he was here in a way, helping them catch the wild horses.

Steck was already asleep, breathing deep.

Correen knew she should have been tired, too, but instead she was anxious. The outlaws were running loose while Little Crow lay in his grave. They had all taken part in murdering the boy. She wanted them all dead. The black man, the other redhead, and especially Ike Lafferty. If her late husband had taught her one thing, it was how to hate a man.

But these were good men in her company, if strange. Bob Steck: gentlemanly yet violent. Wolverton: struggling with bloodshed and righteousness. Boyish in a way, seeking a mother's affection.

And Claude, the strangest of all. Running from something? Restless? Haunted. Could he truly so love a friend that he would grieve still for this dead man, this Dusty Sanderson? Still seeking vengeance after eleven years? He wasn't as tough as he let on. She had seen his face, horrified, when the Sickle twin swung between them, and she had felt the same way.

Maybe they were more alike than she cared to admit. Maybe, eleven years from now, she would still be plotting Ike Lafferty's death.

What would happen when this was over? After she took her revenge on Lafferty, would she stand and watch Claude take his on Lone Wolf? Even if she understood Claude's hatred, she didn't want to see Wolverton die. Something about the old murderer charmed her. Something rare and sincere.

She shook her head—she might not live to worry about it. It wasn't her business, anyway. These men—these big strong fools—would do what they wanted in the end.

She kept the fire burning small but hot until she heard Wolverton slogging across the shallow creek. The big man put the Winchester down beside the Creedmoor and began pulling his boots off. "I don't see anybody on our trail," he said. He got one boot free and put it near the fire to dry. While pulling the second one off, the Creedmoor caught his eye again, and he stared at it as a drunk would a bottle of whiskey.

"It's not a snake, you know," Correen said. "It won't bite."

"Like hell it won't," he said as his boot came

free. Then he looked at her, embarrassed. "Pardon my language, but it bites, all right."

"So will any other weapon. What's different about that one?" She watched as he unwrapped a square of wet cloth from each foot. Two different fabrics in different prints. He wrung them out and draped them over his boot tops. "It makes me smell blood again," he said, stretching his feet toward the fire. "It tempts me."

"To kill?"

He nodded, looked at the long rifle again. He reached for it, put his hand around the breech. "Like nobody knows." He lifted the gun, snapped it to his shoulder. His eyes grew wet looking down the barrel, until he squinted them shut. He put the Creedmoor across his lap. "I'd sooner hold the devil's pitchfork, but I guess I'd better get used to it in case we need it."

Correen added a branch to the fire. "How did it start, Mr. Wolverton? The killin'?"

The big man shrugged. "When I was a kid in Indian Territory, I got the idea I wanted to kill somebody one day. I don't know why. The Indian in me, maybe. Maybe the white man. Maybe the devil. I figured there wasn't any harm in it, as long as I picked somebody who deserved to die."

The water was steaming out of one boot, so he moved it a little farther from the fire.

"You went lookin' for someone to kill?"

"You might say so. A lot of outlaws in the territory then. Bounties on 'em. I went to Fort Smith, Arkansas, collected some Wanted posters, and went huntin'. I was seventeen when I killed my first outlaw. Tracked him to his camp. Waited for him to finish cookin' his biscuits and beans. Shot him in the back, then ate his supper."

"Just as you shot Dusty Sanderson?"

Wolverton sighed. "That was a couple of dozen corpses later, but it all led to that. The devil's work, and I enjoyed every second of it, and every drop of blood I spilt, till I shot the wrong man."

Correen shook her head as if annoyed at the big man. "How could you have made such a mistake?"

"Killin' had gotten casual with me," he said, his face staring blankly. "I got careless about it. Some ranchers had hired me to kill a rustler name of Giff Dearborn. I came across a fellow who looked like Giff from afar, but didn't even bother to get close enough to make sure. I just shot him in the back, and like Duval says, left him lay in his own fire, puttin' that cartridge shell in his hand. Later, when I found out I'd killed the wrong man, I finally saw myself for what I was."

They sat in silence beside the fire. Wolverton turned the rags draped over his boots until they had dried all over. Correen pitied him for some reason and yet admired him. She tried to hate him like Claude did, but couldn't.

Bob Steck began to snore.

"I didn't know Dusty, but he was my own personal savior," Lone Wolf finally said. "Just like Jesus, he died for my sins, so I could know what it really means to live. God bless his soul, and save mine. I'm a sinner, Correen. I'd go to hell if it wasn't for Jesus Christ and Dusty Sanderson."

She watched him wrap the rags back around

his feet, working with nimble familiarity as a woman might tie up her hair. He tucked the loose corners in under his arches and caught her curious eyes. "California socks," he said, smiling. "The only kind I've ever worn."

She smiled as she rose. She fetched another branch for the fire, pausing to put her hand on Wolverton's shoulder. She didn't know why. She felt he needed it.

Hoofbeats came from downstream and Wolverton lifted the Creedmoor before he could recognize Claude on Casino. Correen pulled away from the big man, stroked back a strand of hair blowing across her face.

"You got friendly with that gun quick," the regulator said, pivoting on the stirrup. He had a piece of his shirttail wrapped around his right hand.

The new voice in camp woke Steck.

"Sorry," Lone Wolf said, lowering the long barrel. "Didn't know it was you."

"That's all right," Claude said, kicking Lone Wolf's boots aside so he could stand at the fire. "I know you wouldn't shoot a man who was lookin' you in the eye. That's not your style."

Correen's eyes scolded him for antagonizing the big man. "What's wrong with your hand?" she asked.

"Nothin'."

Steck sat up on the ground. "Then what the hell did you bandage it for?"

"I boogered it up a little, that's all. Anything to eat in this camp?"

"I'll make you somethin' after I doctor that hand," Correen said, taking him by the wrist.

"Mr. Wolverton, will you fetch a pot of water to boil, please?"

"God A'mighty," Claude groaned. "You'd think I was sick as a thousand head of sheep."

Steck came to look at the hand as Correen unwrapped the dirty bandage. "Boogered it up a little, huh?" the Texan said. "I'd hate to see the booger."

Claude grimaced for several minutes as Correen cleaned the wound, pulling the loosened skin back and forth to examine it, getting every speck of dirt out. She boiled the bandages, dressed the wound in pork fat, and wrapped it again.

"Now I'll cook you a fine tightener," she said when she was done.

"Hell, I've lost my appetite."

"You'll get it back when you smell food. Try not to use that hand for several days. Keep your fingers straight, or you'll pull the wound open again."

"I'm afraid I can't do that, Correen," Claude said, trying to make a fist with his right hand.

"Why not?"

"Because we've got some horses to break."

Twenty-two

Ike Lafferty turned his horse into the corral and walked toward his front porch. The Laramie Plains felt stifling hot compared to the mountains where he had risen before dawn. He was tired of this, but it wasn't half over yet. He would be back in the saddle before noon.

"Emmett!" he shouted as he approached the house. "Emmett, where the hell are you?"

The foreman opened the front door and stepped out, a cup of coffee in his hand. "Howdy, boss," he said nervously. "You back?"

"Emmett, why in the hell are you sittin' around here this time of day, drinkin' coffee?" He stomped up onto the porch and glared at his top hand.

The foreman pointed his thumb over his shoulder and grinned sheepishly. "Sleepin' off a drunk," he said. "How did it go up there?"

"It didn't go worth a damn. They killed Wiloughby, the squaw, and one of the Sickle boys."

Emmett's jaw dropped. "Which one?"

"What damn difference does it make?"

"Frank owes me fifty dollars. Unless it was Clay, sayin' he was Frank. They'll do that sometimes, you know."

"Shut up, Emmett. Did a fellow named Wolverton ride through here after I left?"

"Yes, sir. Lone Wolf."

"Then why the hell didn't you and some of the boys ride up with him to help me?"

"You said when you left you could handle 'em better alone."

"That was before Wolverton joined 'em. You know who he is?"

"Yes, sir."

"Then why didn't you ride up with him and give me a hand?"

"Well, I didn't know exactly who he was at the time. He just said he was lookin' for Bob Steck to give him a message from Texas."

Lafferty put his hands on his hips. "But you know who he is now?"

"Yes, sir."

"How did you happen to find out who he was after he left?" the rancher asked, glowering, his head jutting forward on his neck.

"I told him," a voice said from the house. A stranger stepped onto the porch, a cup of coffee in one hand, a sweat-stained felt hat in the other. He stood about five-ten, spare, a balding scalp leaving an island of hair perched over his forehead. He seemed proud of it, having gathered it and combed it into a curl. His eyes seemed bottomless, like two cups of black coffee, sprouting red veins this morning. He wore a sheepskin vest, a revolver belted high on his hip, brown corduroys worn slick at the knees.

"Who are you?" Lafferty asked.

The stranger pressed his hat on the back of his head, leaving the lone curl in view. He shifted his coffee cup to his left hand. "Giff Dearborn," he said, thrusting his right hand toward the rancher. "It's my fault Emmett got drunk last night. I brought the whiskey."

Lafferty shook the man's hand, turning the name over several times in his head. "What brings you around here?"

"Lone Wolf."

"What do you want with him?"

Dearborn slurped his coffee. "A clean shot." He grinned.

Lafferty took his hat off and scratched his head, squinting at the stranger. Suddenly, the name engaged a cog in his memory. "You're the rustler Lone Wolf thought he killed when he shot Dusty Sanderson."

"That's right," Dearborn said. "Nothin' makes me madder than somebody shootin' me dead. Even if I don't turn out to be me."

Emmett laughed, sloshed his coffee, and rubbed at a deep piercing pain over his right eye.

Lafferty smirked. "Lone Wolf's got three others with him up there. All sure shots, even though one's a woman. I wouldn't go after 'em alone if I was you."

Dearborn shuffled his boots, looked far out across the Laramie Plains. "I couldn't help overhearin' what you were sayin' just before I stepped out. Sounds like your Snowy Range Gang has just about been wiped out."

"Snowy Range Gang?" Lafferty said.

"Emmett told me all about it last night," Dearborn explained. "His tongue gets looser the more he drinks."

Lafferty shot an angry glance at his foreman.

"Tell you what," Dearborn suggested. "You help me get Wolverton, and I'll help you with the other three. Then we'll put a new Snowy Range Gang together and take to tradin' stock."

Lafferty frowned, but inside his spirits lifted. He had not been looking forward to facing Wolverton, Duval, Steck, and the woman with just a handful of cowboys. Giff Dearborn looked like a godsend standing on his front porch, if God could send a devil. This Dearborn was no idiot blowhard like Wild Roy Wiloughby, but a serious customer with experience.

"You still carry a runnin' iron?" Lafferty said.

Dearborn licked his fingers and twisted the curl on his crown as if it were a mustache. "I haven't carried one in a few years, but I haven't forgot how to improve a brand with one, either. I could practice on those humpbacked bulls you've got out there."

"What kind of business have you been in lately?"

"Gravel."

"Huh?"

"Minin' it from boulders."

Emmett laughed. "He pulled the same one on me last night! Said he's been a *guest* of the state of Colorado."

"I had a damn fine position there," Dearborn said. "The state give me three square meals a day, though the squares was awful small, a suit of striped clothes, a blanket, a hammer, and even some jewelry to wear. But I decided to take my leave when I heard about Wolverton's pardon in Texas."

"He escaped," Emmett said, patting the outlaw on the shoulder. "Knocked a guard's head in with a sledgehammer, stole his horse, and rode hell for leather!"

"I just missed Wolverton in Texas," Dearborn added. "Trailed him up here."

Lafferty could not hold his grin back any longer. "Mr. Dearborn—Giff—I'm in need of a man like you. You help me clean Wolverton and his bunch out of my mountains, and I believe we can go partners in this territory."

"Well, then," Dearborn said, taking his hat off, "if you don't mind me invitin' you into your own house, why don't you tell me what we're up against over a cup of coffee." He kicked the door open, bowed, and gestured toward the doorway with his brim.

Twenty-three

❦

The afternoon sun shone into the canyon bright and warm where frost had sparkled this morning. Claude breathed a sigh of relief when he saw the barricade still intact, the mustangs milling nervously inside. The thought of the gray stallion coming back to rescue his mares had dogged him the whole time he was gone.

The wild horses stampeded around the bend to the head of the canyon when he began taking the section out of the barricade. After leading Casino in, he replaced the rails and brush, untied a lariat from his saddle string, and swung a loop in it. He rode up the left side of the canyon, the noose ready at his right leg.

When the lead mare saw him come around the bend, she tried to climb the canyon walls, her eyes rolling with fear. The other horses panicked, scattering. Claude let the mare with the foal run by, then spurred Casino to cut off the second mare, a sleek bay with a white face. He whirled his loop twice, threw it as the mare balked, saw it hit her neck and flip around her head.

The bay hit the end of the short lariat, tied fast to the saddle horn. Hemp stretched and leather squeaked, but everything held. Casino had the advantage in size and strength, turning his rump to the roped mare, pulling her toward the mouth of the canyon.

The other two horses stampeded down from the head of the canyon, and the lead mare hit the rope stretched between Casino and his catch. For a moment, Claude thought he would see a bad tangle, then the lead mare jumped, the rope catching her hooves and throwing her. She grunted as she hit, squealed, and jumped to her feet again, uninjured.

Claude tried to keep a tight rope on the bay, but she was dodging, trying to shake the loop around her throat. The twists of hemp whirred against pine saplings, the mare stupidly wrapping herself around every slender tree trunk that came between her and the big paint. Claude wondered how Little Crow had intended to handle this part, roping his wild horse afoot.

As he worked the mustang toward the mouth of the canyon, tediously unwrapping her from trees, he saw the lead mare prancing along the barricade, gathering herself repeatedly for a jump she never took. He decided to avoid looking at her, afraid he would see her lead the other mares in escape. As Casino pulled the darting bay near the barricade, the other mustangs charged again toward the head of the canyon.

The bay would not go near the one tree Claude wanted her to wrap around—a sapling standing a few yards away from the pole fence. After several minutes of maneuvering, he finally forced his catch to wind herself around the trunk, with only a few feet of slack. She shook needles from the sapling, jerking against the rope.

Casino leaned against the lariat, keeping it tight, as Claude climbed down. He took an old rope from the cantle strings, tied a bowline in one end. He worked his way around to the side of the roped bay, tossed the bowline under her neck. Then he tossed the other end of the rope over her withers. Staying clear of her hooves, he moved around to her other side and gathered both ends of the rope he had tossed over and under her neck. He ran one end through the bowline on the other end and quickly drew the new noose tight.

This second rope Claude wrapped around one of the trees supporting Little Crow's barricade. He wrapped it low, three feet from the ground, taking just one turn around the tree before tying the rope off at a third tree.

The mare was roped twice now, tied to two different trees. Claude got back on Casino, spurred him forward a few steps, and untied the lariat from the saddle horn. It was his best rope, and he wanted to use it to catch the other horses. He let the mare pull away from the first tree, then got down and went to his second rope. Every time the bay took a step toward the fence, Claude took another foot of slack out of the rope. In a few minutes, he had her tied close to the fence. The fence would keep her from wrapping herself around a tree and strangling herself. The rope was wrapped low so that even if she fell, she wouldn't choke.

The mare seemed ready to die of fright when Claude reached through the fence to take his good lariat from her head. He spoke to her in a low voice, trying to calm her, but she rammed the fence several times before he could catch the loop and pull it over her ears.

He coiled his lariat and mounted Casino again. He hoped to have two more mares caught and tied by the time Correen and the others arrived on foot. The thought of her keeping company with Lone Wolf all this time bothered him. He had seen her hand on the big man's shoulder when he came back to camp. But it was probably better this way. He was doing something useful, carrying the fight against Ike Lafferty and his cutthroats. Lone Wolf wouldn't even agree to shoot at the bastards unless they shot first.

He had never thought of settling down with a woman before, but now it felt as if the idea had always been with him. He was going to bust up this Ike Lafferty bunch, get Steck's cattle back, and take up with Correen. He was thinking way ahead, and that wasn't good, but he couldn't help himself.

He was trotting back up the canyon when he felt Dusty Sanderson riding beside him—only a momentary lapse, but it felt as certain as if they had never been broken apart.

He had forgotten something: kill Wolverton.

Twenty-four

∽∾

Claude was fighting the lead mare when the three hikers arrived at the mustang trap. He had decided not to rope the mare with the foal, thinking the little one might get in the way. The lead mare, older and more set in her ways, would prove ornery, but could be broken.

Wolverton crawled through the brush and roped the big mare a second time, using his lariat to draw the horse up to the fence. A third mare, a rather poor-looking claybank, was already tied some distance away.

"All right, you're such an expert," Claude said. "Show us how the Indians break 'em." He loosened the end of the rope from his saddle horn and dropped it.

"Looks like you know about as much as I do," Wolverton replied. "You started out like I would've." He looked over the lead mare for a minute or two, then walked to the other two horses, judging them. "I'll work the big one," he finally said. "Bob, you take that little claybank. Sabinal, you get the bay."

"I've told you not to call me that," Claude said, staking Casino to graze.

Steck plowed through the barricade, spooking the mares. "How come you give me the scrawny one?"

"For goodness' sake," Correen said, her voice knifing through the brush. "Stop bickerin' among yourselves and break the horses!" She began setting up a camp in the mouth of the canyon.

"She's right," Wolverton said. "Now, the first thing you do is get a second rope on your mare around the base of her neck. The safe way to do it is to tie a bowline in the end of a rope, throw it under her neck, and—"

"I know how to do it!" Claude snapped.

"I don't!" Steck said.

Wolverton helped the rancher get the second rope on the claybank. The little horse fought when the end of the rope flew over her withers, but she could go nowhere.

"Stay away from her feet, Bob," Wolverton said. "Especially those front ones. She'll put one over your shoulder before you know it and stomp you down." He watched Steck bend over to pick up the end of the rope, noticing that the old Texan's right knee wouldn't bend. That leg he had been favoring all day must be hurting bad.

Wolverton went back to the lead mare and picked up the rope lying on the ground beside her. Keeping the rope tight, he swung around behind the horse, letting the rope slap against her left shoulder, flank, and hip. The mare shied every time the rope touched her, pulling hard against the fence.

"They think that rope's gonna hurt 'em," he explained. "Just let 'em fight it for a while. They'll get used to it."

When the mare had settled down some, the big man let the rope sag along her back left leg and rub against her cannon and ankle. She kicked at it until she had stepped over it, then Wolverton drew it up tight between her thighs. The mare came near tearing the tree she was tied to out by the roots.

"You call this breakin' 'em?" Steck said. "Looks more like you're tryin' to loco 'em to me."

"She's just a little skittish," Wolverton said. "It's like somebody tyin' you up hand and foot and droppin' a chicken snake in your shirt. Drive you crazy for a few minutes, then you'd get used to it and could carry a snake in your shirt like a money belt if you wanted to."

Claude followed Wolverton's example with his white-face bay, laughing at the mustang's wild contortions with the rope between her legs.

"Now, keep the rope up high between her legs," Wolverton directed, "and swing back around to her neck." He showed them how, keeping the rope pulled tight around the back of the mare's left thigh. "Stick the end of your rope through the noose around her neck. Watch those hooves!" He pulled the rope end through and drew it tight, making a loop around the mare's back left leg.

"Now watch," he said. "Let the loop drop

down to her fetlock, but keep it tight. When she steps or kicks, draw it tighter, pullin' her leg up off the ground." He hauled in the rope as he explained, cinching the mare's leg up several inches from her belly. "Pull hard," he said, gritting his teeth as he fought the rope, "because she'll try to kick and get a rope burn around the back of her ankle if you let the rope slip." He tied it off to the noose around her neck and turned to watch the other two men.

"Now, Bob," he said, "you don't have to watch out for those hooves anymore. She can't rear up to paw on just one back leg. Can't kick, either."

"The worst she can do now is fall on you, Bob," Claude added.

"I'll bet she can still bite, too."

"When you get a foot tied up," Wolverton said, "you two come on over here and we'll all three work 'em over real good one at a time. Grab a saddle and a blanket."

Claude brought the saddle and Steck limped over with the blanket.

"All right, Bob, I want you to start rubbin' the blanket all over her. Start on her neck and go easy, then get a little rougher. Then throw it on and off of her all over. Don't hurt her with it because I want her to learn that it won't hurt her, but work up to slappin' it against her until she's used to it."

Steck started rubbing the blanket on the shivering mare's neck.

"Duval, just pick that saddle up every now and then and drop it," Wolverton suggested. "Then flap it around a little."

"What are *you* gonna do?" Claude said. "Watch?"

"No, I'm gonna run a rope around her legs so she'll get used to that and won't panic if she ever gets tangled. Now, let's work her over real good."

For several minutes they rubbed the mare with the blanket, shook saddle and straps at her, ran ropes around her legs.

"Usually, you'd do all this to her one thing at a time," Wolverton said, "but we're hard up for time. She's no outlaw, anyway. She'll be all right." He backed off and threw his rope at her head, over her neck, over her back.

"You let that leg down and she's liable to turn outlaw," Steck said. He walked around her rump, rubbing the blanket on her, lifting it and letting it fall.

"Naw, she's fine," Wolverton replied. "I've seen 'em so bad you'd have to draw both legs up like that and throw 'em on the ground to work 'em. This old hoss ain't no trouble. Duval, press that saddle against her now, shake it around. Rub that cinch under her belly."

"I'm workin' up to that," Claude said.

In half an hour the big mare was covered with sweat, but she had stopped pulling against the rope tying her to the fence and was breathing easier.

"Bob, put the blanket on," Lone Wolf said. "Duval, you throw the saddle on and off a few times."

"Do it yourself," Claude said, dropping the saddle at Wolverton's feet. "I'm gonna get a bridle."

He walked down the fence to the place where

he and Steck had pushed all the riding tack through the brush in the barricade. He picked up a bridle and looked for Correen through the gap in the brush. She had stretched a rope between two trees and thrown a tarp over it to make a tent, in case the weather turned wet again. He searched until he found her, climbing the northern canyon wall, a Winchester in her hand.

Claude grunted his approval and couldn't help grinning a little. That woman beat any he had ever seen, standing guard so the men could play with horses.

Wolverton had thrown the saddle on and off several times and was cinching it down when Claude got back with the bridle. Before climbing on, the big man put some weight on the saddle seat with his hands, then his elbows, finally pulling his feet off the ground. The mare pranced a little but couldn't move much with just three legs under her.

The big man stepped into the stirrup then and mounted as if the mare had been ridden a thousand times. She craned her neck and humped her back but was too tired to make trouble. Wolverton got down after just a few seconds, then got back on again. He stayed longer, shifted his weight. He climbed up and down a dozen times before he was through.

"Let's put that bridle on her," he said. "Then we'll let her foot down so she can rest, and go work with the others."

Claude eased the headstall over the mare's ears, slipped the bit between her teeth. She didn't like the feel of the metal in her mouth but could do nothing about it.

Claude removed the bridle reins so the mare wouldn't step on them and break them off, and Wolverton lowered her hind foot to the ground.

"She'll make a good mount," the big man said as they started toward the little claybank.

"If she'll rein," Steck said. "I don't know that a mustang will learn to rein in two days."

"That'll be a problem, but we'll train 'em as best we can," Wolverton said. He looked through the brush at the camp. "Where's Correen?"

"On the canyon rim, standing guard," Claude said. He stopped and looked toward the point of rocks above.

"I don't see her," Steck said, shading his eyes.

"You sure she's up there?" Wolverton added.

"I saw her headin' that way with a rifle."

They saw Correen rise from the rocks, wave at them, and disappear again. All three men waved back.

"That's a heck of a gal," Wolverton said, an admiring grin on his face.

Claude lowered his arm and glowered at the big man, his upper lip curling.

"Oh, hell," Steck groaned, catching the look on Claude's face. "All we need now is for you two short-trigger men to go sweet over the same damn woman."

Twenty-five

~o~

Sickle couldn't remember ailing a day in his life, ruling out hangovers. But now he had hot spells that made him sweat, chills that made him shiver. He felt stiff all over. He was tired of riding, looking. He wanted to roll up in a blanket and sleep. "I don't think he come this way," he said. "We've cut every trail headin' west, and there ain't a track one."

"Where else would he go?" Squaw Man said, leaning on his saddle horn. Early this morning, he had snuck near enough to the tepee under the Snowy Range to count heads. He had seen the woman at the fire, Wolverton and Steck drinking coffee. But Duval had slipped away in the night on the big paint stallion, and all trails were covered with melting slush. He had assumed that Duval was riding west to find help in North Park.

"Maybe we should split up," Sickle suggested. "I'll keep lookin' for his trail this way, and you go back to their camp, see if he came back. Hell, he may have just gone out for a scout." He pulled his coat tight around his neck, the chills coming on again, shivering him in his own sweat.

"Don't know where else he'd go," Squaw Man said. "Ain't nothin' to the south or north. He wouldn't go east, chance runnin' onto Ike."

"That's what I say!" Sickle growled. "Either I'll find his trail headin' west or you'll find him back at their camp."

Squaw Man shifted in the saddle, rubbed his chin. "All right, you look over here the rest of the day. If you find his tracks, go after him. If you don't, come back tomorrow and meet me where we camped last night."

Sickle nodded.

Squaw Man reined east and started back toward the Snowy Range. When he had gone, Sickle got down, unsaddled and hobbled his horse, rolled himself in a blanket, and went to sleep.

It was late in the afternoon when Squaw Man saw the tip of the meat pole through the treetops. He approached carefully but expected to find no living souls around the deserted camp of the old Snowy Range Gang. He heard hooves and turned to see the bremmer cattle grazing around two fresh graves.

As he sat in the saddle, wondering which grave held his squaw, he spotted the scaffold in the tree by the creek. Strange that they should bury her the Cheyenne way. Then he remembered hearing that Wolverton had some Indian blood. He must have done it out of some tribal superstition.

Trotting to the scaffold, he rode under it, took hold of a limb, and pulled himself up. His pocketknife cut the rawhide thongs around the old buffalo robe. He unwrapped the hide, found Strikes the Dog's eyes open, her mouth gaping. He tried to close them, but the corpse was rigid. He counted three bullet holes in her chest and many more places where buckshot had hit her. At least they hadn't hanged her.

An hour later, he reached the base of the Snowy Range, left his horse in a thicket of scrub oak, and began sneaking toward the tepee beside the lake. When it came into view over a ridge, he sat down to watch. It seemed abandoned, but he had to make sure.

He moved closer, thinking it might be a trap to lure him into the open. He could imagine Wolverton waiting in the rocks across the lake, the long Sharps Creedmoor in his hands. It wouldn't be a difficult shot for an expert. Maybe four hundred yards. The bullet could go damn near through four sheep.

He stopped a couple of hundred yards away and studied the camp. Everything but the tepee was gone. Of course, they could have put everything inside to fool him. Maybe they were waiting inside themselves. He wanted badly to hike down there and see, but the thought of ambush held him back.

For several minutes he planned his approach. He would dodge from this tree to that, remaining shielded from shots fired across the lake.

When he had every step memorized, he skulked closer, holding his rifle ready before him.

The last ten paces were the most dangerous. Nothing to shield him as he ran to the entrance hole of the lodge. But the flap was open, and he could see inside. He sprinted across the open ground and leaped in.

A few blankets. An iron pot. Some unused firewood. Cool ashes. They had taken everything they could carry on their backs. Had Duval stranded them? No, not the sort. He remembered the regulator risking his life to cut the Indian boy loose yesterday.

He sat down to think. Yesterday he had watched from a distance as they hauled their saddles up from the outlaw camp below. Now the saddles were gone. Why would they carry their saddles on their backs unless they expected to get some horses somewhere?

The vision of the steel-gray stallion galloped across the hide wall of the lodge. Squaw Man remembered finding the trap the Ute boy had built in the canyon to the north. Strikes the Dog had planned to use it to catch the wild horses after making the boy her slave. Were they going to try to ride wild horses out of the mountains?

Squaw Man stepped out of the tepee, looking for tracks, oblivious to the thought of ambush now. He found footprints along the lake at the base of the Snowy Range. Long strides in a straight line. They knew where they were going and wanted to get there quick. The tracks pressed deep in the mud, even the woman's, though she couldn't have weighed over a hundred pounds by herself. They were carrying heavy loads. Steck was limping. Maybe he really

had injured his leg jumping from the bluff yesterday morning. Something had dragged beside
him here. A cinch buckle?

Yes, he had them figured now. Duval had ridden around the Snowy Range in the night, then
headed north to find the mustang trap. The others had followed this morning on foot. They
were desperate for horses.

He turned back for his mount. He would find
them tomorrow, see how they had fared with
the mustang trap, then ride to warn Lafferty. He
wouldn't let them get away. He wanted them
alive. He wanted to know which one had killed
his woman.

Sickle woke in the middle of the night, suffo-
cating. He sat up, gasping for breath as if someone had knocked his wind out in his sleep. But
he was alone. He had dreamed of nothing but
blackness. A chill shivered him. Then he felt the
call. Neither name nor voice, but a cool grip, a
tortured plea.

He found his horse nearby, put the bridle on,
took the hobbles off. He saddled up and rode.

At dawn he reached the abandoned outlaw
camp, his head throbbing with pain, his skin
burning as if scalded. Somehow, he knew where
to look, finding two mounds, rock-covered,
marked with sorry crosses. He fell on one and
raked the dirt and rocks back until his hands
were bleeding. Day broke as he felt a handful of
cloth and hauled up with all his strength, un-
earthing the body. The light of day struck his
face as he unwrapped the death shroud.

It was like finding his own corpse, robbing his
own grave. The crick in his neck knifed him

with new pain, and his limbs stiffened. He looked up and saw the humpbacked cattle in a line, staring at him, their short black horns jutting. He was tired, cold in his own sweat, weak. He lay down beside the body of his brother and went to sleep.

Twenty-six

❧

Claude rode the bay mare back to the fence Little Crow had built, pulling wide on the reins to turn the green-broke mount. "Hell, she didn't hardly buck at all," he said, his boots hitting the ground. The mustang wore streaks of lather from the thirty-minute ride.

Wolverton was sitting on Casino, ready to chase down the bay had she thrown Duval. "I figured the lead mare for the worst outlaw," he said.

"That explains the fact of her landin' you on your ass," Steck said, chuckling. He was throwing his saddle on and off of the scrawny claybank. "I think this one's ready now. She don't even flinch anymore when this old kack lands on her."

"Then get on," Claude suggested.

Steck cinched the saddle down, mounted and

dismounted several times. "Yeah, she's ready. Poor thing's already plumb wore out."

He untied the rope around her back left foot, letting her get four hooves under her. Claude removed the rope from the mare's head and held her by the ears as Steck climbed once more into the saddle.

"Let her buck!" the old rancher said.

Claude released the mare's head and backed away, but she merely stood there, spraddle-legged, confused.

"Touch her with the spurs," Wolverton said. "Not hard."

When she felt the steel against her ribs, the pony flinched and took a few awkward steps. Steck poked her again, and she began to walk. "Look at that!" Steck shouted over his shoulder. "By God, a three-year-old could ride this hoss!"

Wolverton followed on Casino. "See if she'll stop."

The Texan pulled back on the reins. "Whoa," he said, and the mare stopped, twisting her head against the bit in her mouth. "This ain't no mustang," he said. "That silver stud must have stolt this mare from a farm somewhere."

Claude picked up a rock. "If you want her to buck, Bob, I can oblige you."

Steck started the mare walking again. "I didn't say that." He rode the claybank slowly, a hundred yards up the canyon. "I can feel her humpin' her back all up. What do you reckon that means?"

Wolverton was following on Casino. "Hard to say. See if she'll rein."

Steck pulled the right rein wide and the claybank followed the bit in her mouth. "I'm tellin' you she's been rode before," he said.

"Her back still humped up?"

"No, she quit that. This is some kid's saddle horse, Lone Wolf." He put the spurs to her ribs, and the claybank leaped forward, trotting toward the barricade.

"Looks like you got shortchanged," Claude shouted as the horse and rider came toward him. "Want to ride mine next time?"

"Hell, no," Steck said, nonchalantly drawing his reins. "I generally hire boys to buck out my horses. This little nag suits me just—"

The claybank jerked her head down between her front legs, kicked her hind legs, twisted, sent Steck flying, then went to hopping around the canyon on all fours.

Claude brought his knee up, slapped it, and laughed as Wolverton chased down the claybank on Casino. The regulator helped the stiff-legged rancher to his feet. "What happened to your saddle horse, Bob?"

"She jumped astraddle of her head and like to broke in two, damn her. Bring her back over here, Lone Wolf, and let me settle the score!"

Wolverton led the claybank back to Steck, and Claude grabbed her by the ears to keep her still. The rancher mounted again, swinging his stiff right leg over the cantle.

"All right, Sabinal, let her go."

The claybank ducked her head again, but this time Steck was ready. He leaned back in the saddle and fought her head with the reins. She whirled, bowing her neck to the left, kicking her hind legs to the right. With his right leg in pain, the Texan had trouble hooking his knees under the swells of the saddle, and he lost his right stirrup. The mare seemed to sense it and jumped to the left, dumping the rider.

Claude helped Steck up from the ground again. "That bum leg's foulin' you up, Bob. Let me buck her out for you."

"Like hell. Bring her back, Lone Wolf!"

Wolverton led the claybank back to Steck, smiling. "Before you get on again, I want to show you a trick," he said, getting down from Casino. He fetched a piece of old rope from the fence and tied one end of it to the ring on the left side of the claybank's bridle bit. "Now, you run this rope up the bridle and through the headstall," he said, threading the rope as he explained. "Then you take the rope back to the saddle horn, wrap it around once, and go back to the other side of the bridle."

He threaded the rope down the right side of the bridle, as he had come up the left side. Then he tied the end to the right-hand ring in the bit and cut the excess rope off. "We'll use this piece to make sure that loop doesn't slip off the saddle horn." He tied the leftover length of rope just in front of the horn, securely linking the bridle and saddle together.

"The bit will keep her from duckin' her head too low," Wolverton explained. "Somebody's grandmother could ride her now."

Steck smirked at the strange bridle rig but put his foot in the stirrup to try again. "I ain't nobody's grandmother, but I'll try, anyway."

Claude gave the claybank her head, and she attempted a buck but pulled up short and stood testing the new restraint. Steck spurred her, and she kicked a little but couldn't put much into it with her head trussed up.

"That knee's botherin' him worse than he lets on, ain't it?" Wolverton said as Steck rode away on the mustang.

"He wouldn't complain if it was busted clean off," Claude replied. He heard the big man chuckle and started to smile himself but remembered whom he was talking to.

Twenty-seven

꩜

Claude sucked bacon grease from the fingers of his left hand as Correen inspected his right. At least this time she had waited until after he ate before she went to poking at his wound.

"Your fingers are a bit puffy, Mr. Duval." She unbuttoned his sleeve and rolled it up. Turning his wrist up, she found the beginnings of a red streak reaching toward his elbow. "It's infected." She pursed her lips and began removing the bandage.

"I'll get some more water to boil," Wolverton said, leaving camp with a small pot.

When he returned from the creek, the big man had the pot in one hand, a bundle of greenery in the other. "Try this," he said to Correen. "Mash the leaves and stems up together and make a poultice."

"What is it?" Correen asked, taking the plants from Wolverton.

"Wild lettuce."

Claude smirked. "What makes you think that'll help?"

"Horse bit me one time in New Mexico," Lone Wolf said, rubbing his shoulder as if the injury still hurt. "Got infected. Some old medicine woman wrapped it up in some of that wild lettuce. Cleared it up overnight."

Claude rolled his eyes. "Hell, throw some lizard tails and snake tongues in with it." He winced as Correen poked a tender spot on his wound. It was an ugly mess today, red and swollen.

"It couldn't make anything worse," she said, "and might help."

"I wouldn't pass judgment on those old Mexican herb women, Sabinal," Steck said. "One time I was down south of San Antonio buyin' stock to take up the trail, and I got a big ol' boil on my . . ." He rubbed his rear end and glanced toward Correen. "Well, I couldn't ride, it hurt so bad. But this old herb woman down there sold me a mess made of mashed-up pokeberries and red oak bark. By golly, it drew that boil to a head overnight, and I went on about my business."

"I know a thing or two about home remedies myself," Claude argued. "One time up in North Texas, one of the boys got snake-bit. One feller said to put coal oil on it, and another said gunpowder, so they doubled up and put both, and I mean a bunch of it, too. That night the boys built a fire out of some old cedarwood, and you know how that stuff pops when it burns. Well, a spark jumped out of the fire and blew the boy's whole leg off."

"Oh, my Lord," Correen said.

"Kill him?" Steck asked.

"Didn't have to. He was already dead from the snakebite."

Steck broke into laughter.

"Sounds like a tall tale to me," Wolverton said. "Did you see this happen?"

"No, but I talked to some boys that did. It was up on the Four Sixes." He drew his watch just far enough from his vest pocket for a glance.

Correen put the water on to boil and began crushing the wild lettuce.

"You know how the Four Sixes got its name?" Steck asked.

"Poker game," Claude answered, pulling his whiskey flask out with his free hand.

"Now, that is puredee bull . . ."

As they argued, Claude unstoppered his flask and turned it upside down over his mouth. "Correen, didn't you find some whiskey in that outlaw camp?"

"Aye." She dipped a bandage from the boiling water with a knife blade.

"What did you do with it?"

"Didn't I pour it out?" she said, smiling smugly at the regulator.

"Damn," Steck said. "I didn't know a Scot could make a temperance fanatic."

"Maybe that's why they ran her out of the old country," Claude suggested. "Ouch!" he said, taking a jab in the back of his hand.

"Sorry," Correen said, smiling as she arranged the crushed herbs on the wound. "Mr. Wolverton, when will the horses be ready? We wouldn't want to get discovered and pinned down in this canyon."

"They're ready now," Lone Wolf said.

She looked up at him in amazement. "You're not serious."

"Yes, ma'am, I am. You saw us ride 'em this mornin', didn't you? Claude didn't even get thrown. We'd better finish 'em out on the trail if they're gonna be any use to us against Ike and his boys."

"Does that mean you're ready to fight?" Claude asked.

"Like I said before, I'll fight to protect myself or my friends."

"Don't count me as one of 'em," Claude said. He looked into Correen's eyes as she finished tying the bandage around his hand. She was disappointed in him, but what did she expect?

Steck started laughing, slapping his good knee, his guffaws echoing across the narrow canyon.

"What's so damn funny?" Claude demanded.

"I just got a picture of myself ridin' that green claybank through an outlaw gang, tryin' to draw enemy fire so we can get Lone Wolf, here, to fight. I'll eat horse dung if this ain't the damnedest fix I ever got myself into!"

Twenty-eight

❧

Claude squatted to study the elk sign on the ground, finally feeling relaxed after the long ride on the newly broken horse. His Marlin rested across his thighs, and a long shank of hair dangled from his hat as he pushed his fingers into one of the tracks. Two young bulls, trotting for cover, last night or this morning.

This was what he had come to Wyoming for. To hunt game, not outlaws. Life sure took its little twists.

"I need practice," the voice said behind him.

Claude looked back toward camp to find the long barrel of the Creedmoor propped on the big man's shoulder. He shook his head. "It'll give our position away."

"I know, but I haven't shot long-range in years. I need to brush up in case I have to use this thing. The mustangs are likely gun-shy, too. We'd better get 'em used to shootin'."

Steck limped up beside Wolverton. "He's got two good points, Sabinal." He was dying to see Lone Wolf use the old Sharps.

Claude scratched his itchy beard and looked at Correen, as if to ask her opinion, but she simply looked away from him and went back to her camp chores. "All right," he said. "Take a few shots before it gets dark." He took it as a good sign. Maybe Wolverton was feeling the urge to fight now.

Their camp was eight miles up Rock Creek from Little Crow's mustang trap. They had left the canyon after dinner, riding their green mounts up a crooked trail, training them to rein at every bend. Now the Snowy Range was again in view, bathed in the reds and pinks of a falling sun.

The mustangs had been tied to a stout rope stretched between two trees and were also hobbled to further discourage escape. The men had found it necessary to tie a foot up when hobbling the lead mare, but now she stood resigned with the others, worn out from the day's work.

"I'll get a couple of hundred yards away from the horses for the first shot," Lone Wolf said, "then I'll move closer. The three of you had better stay with 'em to calm 'em down after I shoot."

"What are you gonna shoot at?" Claude asked.

Wolverton's eyes swept the valley to the north. "That dead pine on that little bluff." He pointed a steady finger on the end of a gangling arm. "That'll be about three hundred yards for the first shot, then four hundred, then five hundred. I'll be satisfied if I can hit it in the middle at five hundred."

"I'd be satisfied if I could just see it good," Steck said, squinting. "I hope some of Ike's boys are watchin' and see you hit it. That'll put the fear in 'em."

"And let 'em know we've got mounts now, too," Claude said. "I had planned that for a surprise."

Wolverton marched two hundred yards downstream and lay down on his stomach. Claude could see him adjusting the rear sight for range and throwing sand in the air to judge windage. The marksman settled in behind the graceful stock and lay like a fallen statue for several long seconds.

The long barrel spouted black smoke. The pine on the bluff splintered chest-high. The blast hit like nearby thunder, electrifying the horse-flesh tied at the hitching rope.

"Easy," Claude said to his bay mustang, stroking the shivering horse on the neck. Steck scratched his claybank, and Correen handled the lead mare. Casino, picketed nearby, merely looked up, grass sticking out of his mouth.

Wolverton strolled closer to camp and lay down again. He made his adjustments for the longer shot, aimed, and slammed another bullet into the dead tree.

He opened the breech to let the long rifle cool as he walked into camp for the third try. He stood and looked at the target for a moment, his face intense. He made a minute adjustment on the long-range sight. Reaching into his pocket, he removed a cartridge and slid it into the breech. He sank to his knees as if ready to pray. Then he lowered himself to his belly and put the rifle against his shoulder.

The blast made the mustangs pull against their ropes, but they fought less now than when the first shot came from down the valley. Chunks sprayed from the dead tree, over a quarter mile away.

Steck gave his claybank a good pat on the neck. "By golly, Lone Wolf, you'll do if we can get you to shoot!"

Claude grunted. "Five hundred yards ain't nothin'. Billy Dixon knocked an Indian off a horse from a mile away at the Battle of Adobe Walls."

"Not quite a mile," Wolverton said, leaning the Creedmoor across a saddle seat. He turned his back, walked away from the gun, and sat on the ground, seemingly exhausted. "About seven-eighths of a mile."

"How do you know?" Claude asked. "Were you there?"

"No. But I went back there with Dixon the year after the battle. He showed me where he was when he shot, and where the Indian fell. I measured it with a wagon wheel. It was short of a mile."

"Back during the war," Steck said, "a Union sharpshooter wounded one of our generals from a mile away. Got him when he stepped out of his tent."

"Captain John Metcalf," Lone Wolf said. "Now, that was a shot of true skill."

"I heard about that," Claude replied. "That Yank had a bunch of soldiers build him a platform to shoot off of, had him a surveyor's transit to find the range, even had a telescope on his rifle. Billy Dixon's shot was better. He didn't have any of that crap. He just drew on experience and Kentucky windage and let her rip."

"But it wasn't skill," Wolverton said. "Dixon himself told me it was nothin' but a scratch shot. It ended the battle, though. I didn't think about it back then, but I believe now that the Good Lord had a hand in that shot. He dwells upon battlegrounds as well as in churches."

Claude scoffed as he came to stand over the big man. "He don't dwell in hell where you're goin'."

Correen jabbed the regulator with an armful of wood she was carrying into camp.

"My savior goes with me wherever I wander, no matter the danger."

Claude rolled his eyes, walked across camp, and collapsed on a saddle blanket.

"I don't know, Lone Wolf," Steck said. "I fought with Terry's Texas Rangers in the war, and I saw some scraps a fellow like that wouldn't get within earshot of."

"A fellow like what?" Wolverton said.

"You know, always prayin' and kneelin' down. A man on his knees wouldn't last long in some of the tight places I've seen."

"You talkin' about Jesus?"

Steck nodded.

Wolverton chuckled and shook his head. "You don't understand who Jesus Christ was. He could get riled and ornery as you, Bob, when he wanted to."

"Like when?" Steck said.

"Like in Jerusalem that time the Good Book tells about. Jesus walked in there one day—he was sort of a circuit preacher then—and he found a lot of people tradin' and swappin' money around the church."

Lone Wolf's eyes caught a spark from the air, and he pulled himself up to a squatting position. "Now, the likes of this church—the Temple, they called it—was somethin' we don't see much of out here in the territories. It was about eight or nine hundred years old, made of stone, cedar, and cypress. Had gold angels in it and bronze columns on the front porch. And all around it was a wall that closed in, I'd say, five or six acres." He spread his arms, indicating the valley floor around him, and his eyes looked as though they could conjure the Temple there.

"If you've ever seen the Palace of the Governors in Santa Fe, or any of them old missions down in San Antone, well, maybe it looked kind of like that. Anyway, Jesus walks in there one day, and here's all these horse traders makin' deals. Now, over here was a herd of sheep," he said, pointing at nothing up the valley. "And over yonder, a big bunch of oxen—maybe fifty yokes of 'em. Another fellow was sellin' doves up against a wall over there. There was manure all over the place, and a lot of folks went barefoot back then."

Correen laughed at Wolverton as the big man stood and shook a foot.

"All this riled Jesus, goin' on in the shadow of the church like that, because these were some rough characters, and the brands on some of the stock was still scabbed over. But the thing that really twisted his tail was the money changers. They had all different kinds of money back then—like we've got dollars and pesos down on the border—and these money changers would swap the different kinds for a cut. And they were generally considered a no-'count bunch of thieves."

Taking immense strides across the campground, Wolverton snatched up a coiled length of rope and unwound it. "Now, Jesus was good with his hands, so he got him some rope and built a whip right quick. He was a carpenter most of his life, so he had a good grip and a strong arm. He galloped into the Temple with his whip—riled like all get-out—and stampeded a herd of sheep."

Lone Wolf whistled the rope around his head and popped it at Claude's heels, causing the mustangs to lunge against the hitching line. "You never heard the likes of blattin' sheep as when he got 'em runnin'. Then he got into a mess of oxen and scattered 'em, and they started the jackasses goin', and busted open the doves' cages, and you'd have thought ball lightning was bouncin' on their rumps the way all them critters lit out of there.

"But Jesus still hadn't got it out of his craw, so he waded in with the money changers and knocked over all their jars of different kinds of money. Then he went to throwin' tables around. Kicked a stool out from under the ol' boy hawkin' the doves. And like I say, these were rough characters, but they got out of the Temple, all right, and the folks who needed to get in there to go to church came in."

Wolverton laughed as he coiled the rope. He shook his head. "Lordy, what a sight . . ."

Claude hated thinking it, but he wanted to hear the big man go on. Then he looked at

Correen, saw her lively eyes smiling at Lone Wolf, and got mad.

"Didn't they have law back then?" Steck asked. "Didn't they get after him?"

The smile dropped from Lone Wolf's face. "Oh, they got after him, all right. Yes, Bob, in the end they sure got after him. Nailed him to that cross."

Claude hissed. "That's almost as bad as shootin' a feller in the back and lettin' him burn in his own fire."

Twenty-nine

‍⌒‍

Dusty used to call it a rustler's moon.
Bright enough to steal cattle by; too dark to
shoot by. Claude watched it slide down the
ragged silhouette of the Snowy Range, remembering, listening to the sounds of the night.

He never understood men who dozed off
standing night guard. Too much going on. Owls
sailing between the trees on silent wings. Wolves
howling. Deer stamping alarms to each other.
Birds calling. Here the wind rustled pine needles
and the creek pulled its waters noisily down the
valley. He trusted his ears in this light.

The three mustangs were still, sleeping on
their feet, he supposed. How did they do that?
Casino's white rump and withers glowed faintly
in the meadow nearby. Bob Steck's snore rattled
from his bedroll.

Then it came: a single thud somewhere up the

slope, in the timber. Casino heard, too. The sparse moonlight caught his mane as his head rose high. Man and horse listened. Claude hooked his thumb over the hammer of the Marlin. Casino tossed his head.

Nothing happened, so they relaxed, Claude settling back against a lodgepole pine, Casino cocking his hip as his head drooped again.

What followed came through the air first, like a wheezing scream, then through the very bedrock of the mountain: a drumroll of hooves. Branches snapped as the wild gray stallion came down for his mares, grunting anger with every stride. He burst into the open, a wayward shadow.

Casino lurched to cut the gray off but hit the end of his picket rope. The mustang charged across the clearing and screamed in the ears of his mares. In the night they looked like a single fantastic beast, the claybank's head and neck rising above the withers of the bay, the gray pawing at the ropes. The line they were tied to shook the two trees like a twister would whip a weed, and their shrill voices split the night air.

"Hey!" Claude shouted, running for the string of mounts. "Get the hell out of here!" He growled and hissed, spooking the tethered mares worse than the gray stud. They broke one end of their rope away from a tree and fought each other for freedom. The lead mare reared, got her leg over the claybank's back. Claude saw a wreck coming, then he heard Casino's charge.

The big paint had pulled his picket pin out of the ground and was coming with his head low like a stalking cat. The gray wheeled away from the mares to meet him. They rushed together

like a couple of locomotives, dodging each other's teeth, slamming their shoulders together.

The bay mare was on the ground now and
trying to get up under the claybank, tangling
her rope around the feet of the others.

Both stallions reared and traded blows with
sharp hooves, the paint's white patches bobbing
like fragments of glowing fury. Claude froze,
awed by their screams, a tingle pricking the
back of his neck.

"Stop them!" Correen said, her warm hand
touching his.

Claude put the Marlin to his cheek. "I can't
see the sights!" he cried. He felt Steck and
Wolverton step up beside him.

The stallions reared and pawed again, the
gray tangling his feet in Casino's halter rope,
jerking the paint forward, off balance. The wild
one came down on the paint's neck, biting him
on the withers. Casino's scream grew to a roar.

"Frighten him away!" Correen said.

"Not now. They're tangled!"

Casino whirled out from under the gray, spinning in a blur of white streaks. The halter rope
tightened around the gray's front hooves and
jerked him down, then the paint's heels stomped
the broad gray flank and the wild stallion rolled.

Claude sensed a skirmish at his side and
turned to see Correen drawing Bob Steck's knife
from his belt scabbard. She ran toward the melee
in the clearing, past the tangle of tethered mares,
into the storm of flying hooves.

"Correen!" Claude yelled, running after her.

As the gray rolled to his feet, Casino kicked
again, catching the wild stallion on the shoulder. The rope tightened between them for an in-

stant, then the gray charged, jabbing the paint behind the ears with his sharp front hooves, hobbled
though they were by the tangled rope. Casino
ducked, snapped his teeth at gray flesh.

Correen rushed between them as they braced
for another clash. She grabbed Casino's halter
and sawed at the rope. Both horses reared, and
the woman rose from the ground between them.
Claude raised the rifle, but the gray circled behind Casino. Their hooves cut the air all around
Correen.

A frayed rope end flew as the horses parted.
Correen let the knife fall and clung to Casino's
halter, swinging like a rag doll in the hand of a
galloping child. The gray shadow bucked and
screamed, snapping at the rope tangled around
his forelegs.

Claude caught the paint first, adding his
weight to Correen's on the halter. When the stallion quit pulling, Claude cocked his Marlin and
turned on the gray. The wild horse had kicked
his feet free of the tangled rope and was bolting
for the timber. Claude swung the barrel around
on him as he faded behind branches and tree
trunks. He let three slugs fly but heard the gray
continue up the slope. There was silence, then a
defiant scream, and the hoofbeats faded.

Steck and Wolverton calmed the mares, the
three horses on their feet now, but still tangled,
pulling nervously against one another.

"You all right?" Claude said, his hand taking
the halter beside Correen's.

"Aye," she said. "I think so."

"What kind of damned fool thing was that to
do?"

She saw his eyes glaring in the moonlight and

tossed her hair back. "Someone had to do something. I could see you weren't going to."

"You have no idea what I was gonna do!" he shouted. "You could have got your pretty little head kicked clean off of your shoulders!"

"But I didn't, did I?"

"By the damnedest luck I've ever seen!"

"I'm not afraid of horses, Mr. Duval, and I'm not afraid of you."

Claude felt warm blood under his palm as he touched Casino's withers. "Look here. Those hooves could have laid your hide back just like this." He soothed the heaving stallion as he checked for more wounds.

"My hide is tougher than you think," she argued. "And my head on tighter than—"

Claude grabbed her by the arm and shushed her. "You hear that?"

They stood for a couple of seconds, then heard the crazed roar of the gray again, somewhere up the mountain.

"What the hell is he doin' now?" Claude asked.

Two shots cracked, not a mile away, and echoed across the valley. A third rang out, giving Claude a bearing.

"Somebody's up there," he said. "One of Ike's boys. Get my bridle, Correen!"

Thirty

❦

Squaw Man looked over his rifle barrel at the huge gray hulk of horseflesh on the ground. "Damn," he said. It had taken three bullets to bring the beast down, still twitching now with the last quivers of life. He would have killed the stallion with one shot if he could have seen his sights. But three. He knew they would be coming after him now.

After all, hadn't he located them before dark by the three shots from the Creedmoor? In fact, he had peeked over the ridge in time to see Lone Wolf fire the last volley, splintering a dead tree five hundred yards away. He had seen the mustang mares tied at the hitching rope. He had retreated a mile or so and made a dry camp, no fire. He would ride in the morning to warn Lafferty that the enemy had horses.

But this gray stallion had ruined everything.

The old boy had turned killer, crazed by the loss of his harem. He had come to kill Squaw Man's gelding, frightening the mount so badly that he had pulled his pin from the ground to run for the timber.

The sound of hooves thumped in the dark forest, the picket rope whirring against a tree trunk. "Come on, boy," Squaw Man said, stepping away from the dead stallion. He whistled and clucked his tongue. He heard the hooves circle his clearing, the gelding unsure. He bent and pulled grass, that the horse might hear him and come to eat a handful.

Now a tree shook in the darkness and the gelding grumbled in confusion.

"Whoa, boy," Squaw Man said. The picket rope was tangled: a stroke of luck. He had to saddle up and run. They would be here any minute. Maybe not all of them, but certainly one. Probably the one called Duval, on his big paint stallion. The others wouldn't want to ride the green mounts in the dark if they could help it.

He spotted the movement in the trees and ran forward. "Easy, boy," he said, his voice lending comfort to the horse. He cut the picket rope and led the mount back to camp at a trot. Hoofbeats were coming already as he grabbed his bridle. Should he stay and fight? No, too dark to see his target in this moonlight. Too close to the enemy camp. Run now, fight in the morning.

He threw the blanket on with one hand, the saddle with the other, fumbled with the cinch as the hoofbeats approached. Duval had good ears. Coming on a beeline. This was going to be close. He jammed his Winchester in the saddle scabbard, buckled his gun belt around his waist, left his bedroll on the ground, and mounted. He jabbed the gelding with his spurs and headed south at a dead run.

Casino planted his hooves and shied when he smelled the stallion, almost wrenching Claude from the saddle. The regulator saw the gray hulk on the ground and drew a revolver. Above the creaking of his own saddle leather, and Casino's heaving for air, he heard the retreating hooves.

Searching the black horizon, he glimpsed the rider against the stars, going over a ridge. He slid his pistol back into its holster and spurred the paint.

At a gallop, the trail was barely visible in the moonlight. He gave Casino his head, leaning low over the mane to avoid tree branches. He topped the ridge the rider had crossed before him, straining to see ahead. Down the grade, the trail opened up into a big park, and at the far side he saw a hint of motion. Nothing more than a shadow flitting into blackness. Still a quarter mile ahead. He knew Casino had the scent now and braced himself for a long run.

He rode until the chase had taken him almost due east of the Snowy Range. Another mile south, and he would fall into the shadow of the pinnacles where not even the rustler's moon would light his way. He ducked his head to keep some limbs from whipping his face and cut his own path down a timbered slope.

He was beginning to think Casino had lost the trail when he caught another glimpse of the rider, struggling to get up a steep grade strewn with deadfalls. He reined in for a look at the terrain. Something compelled him to look west, toward the Snowy Range, into the moonlight, and there he saw the unexplainable.

The sacred Indian bulls stood in a line on the ridge, staring down at him, and the moon revealed a clear path snaking up to them. It would take him out of his way but would prove easier to negotiate than the one the outlaw had chosen.

Claude turned the paint west, spurred him to a gallop. He pulled his hat low over his brow to keep the feeble moon rays from shining directly into his eyes. Reaching high ground, the regulator looked around for the bulls, but they had vanished.

He turned south again and saw the rider pass over the divide ahead of him. Much closer now. Maybe two hundred yards. He had made up a lot of ground, and Casino was probably less winded than the outlaw's horse, who had fought the steeper slope and the fallen trees in his path.

As he leaned back into the chase, he glanced behind him for the bremmers. They had been standing there bigger than life. But, now . . . Gone.

Squaw Man unlimbered his quirt when he saw the big paint almost within shooting range behind him. He would stick to the downhill runs now. He wasn't really sure where he was, looking over his shoulder like this, letting his mount choose the path. Did he know this meadow? That bluff? Hard to say in the dark. And it was getting darker, too. Riding into the shadow of the Snowy Range.

He wasn't lost, of course. The high rocky pinnacles were sure landmarks. But exactly what lay around the next bend or over the next rise—he could not say.

He glanced back again. Damn! Duval making an all-out effort now, wanting to end this thing before they ran into the darkest corner of the range. He looked up at the peaks, haloed by moonlight.

"Stop!" the voice said from behind. "I'll shoot, dammit!"

Shoot at what? The noise? The night? The report came and Squaw Man lay low in the saddle. Damn, he *was* shooting! He looked back, saw a muzzle blast as the next round came. He drew his pistol and fired back, aiming by instinct at the powder flare.

What a ride! He looked ahead, grinning at darkness. His eyes opened wide but he could see nothing. He trusted his mount. The old gelding was still a little spooked—rattled by the gray stallion—but he knew this range well enough. Squaw Man had to trust him to smell the way.

He fired back at another muzzle blast, then heard a bullet sing against a boulder at his side. Duval homing in on him. This wasn't working. Maybe he should stop and fight. Yes, hand-to-hand. See how the Texan fared at close quarters in the dark. The next piece of good ground he found, he would stop.

Keep riding south. Get the moon in view again. Choose your ground. Too dark here. Darker than a cat could see in. The pony running downhill. The stars like jewels in the sunlight.

Duval fired again, but Squaw Man ignored him. Don't give the Texan a target to shoot at.

He couldn't see his horse's ears, but this place felt familiar. He looked up at the Snowy Range. Yes, he recognized the silhouette from this angle. What was this place? He rode blind but felt the terrain around him.

The horse grunted, then Squaw Man smelled it, too. Death. Stinking, rotting death. He remembered Wild Roy with the Creedmoor: four dead sheep. The Indian boy, the bleating voices.

Rocks clattered under his pony's hooves, and the stench welled up around him, sticking like lard in his throat. The odor stung his eyes, useless though they were.

Like a shot he found his place on the mountain, visualized every roll and swell. He jerked back on the reins, but too late. The hooves were silent under him, the great odor engulfing him. He remembered rimrocking the sheep with Wild Roy. He remembered their frightened, bulging eyes and felt his own mocking them. He remembered the way they kicked as they fell, and he flailed his feet free of the stirrups. He remembered their voices and heard them again. "Squaw Maaaan!" Louder now, as he fell to join them. He screamed in terror as the wind roared up at him. It was dark, but he saw them all clearly: looking up at him, their tongues lolling out, voices calling his name.

"Squaw Maaaan! Squaw Maaaan!"

Thirty-one

∽∘∾

U h-oh," Steck said, looking expectantly down at the claybank between his legs.

"What's wrong?" Wolverton asked.

"She's got her back all humped up again. I'd say we've got about thirty seconds before she turns herself inside out."

Wolverton flanked the claybank on the left, riding the big lead mare. Correen moved to the right on Claude's bay mustang.

They had worried all night about the far-off gunshots they heard after Claude rode out in the dark. When the regulator failed to return by daybreak, Correen had insisted on riding, though she would have to mount a green-broke horse. They had found Squaw Man's camp and were following the trail of the chase at a trot, a mile into it now, expecting the claybank to start bucking any second.

The mare suddenly stretched her neck and kicked her hind legs straight back. The rig running from the saddle horn, through the headstall, and to the bit kept her from getting her head down low enough to really buck, but she compensated by rearing and whirling. Steck held his seat until the mare threatened to fall over backward on him, then he bailed out and lost his reins.

Correen hazed the runaway claybank toward Wolverton as the big man angled in and leaned from the saddle to grab a dangling rein. The mustangs lunged against each other for a few seconds, but Lone Wolf talked horse to them, settling them down with a few low grunts.

Steck got up and dusted himself off. "She's had her pitch for the day. She'll ride all right now." He took the rein from Wolverton and climbed back on, grimacing as he swung his stiff right leg over the saddle.

"Correen," Wolverton said, "you handle a wild horse right well."

"You call that pet horse wild?" Steck said. "Let her get astraddle of this outlaw and see who handles what . . ."

Claude stopped as he came over the rise and watched the three riders in the clearing. Steck was gesturing, pointing one finger in the air as he spoke. Wolverton was next to Correen, patting her on the back. It riled Claude, and he took it out on Casino, jabbing the big paint with his spurs.

Every time he came back to camp, he found Lone Wolf trying to sweet-talk Correen, now going so far as to reach out and touch her. While he was off chasing outlaws, Lone Wolf was courting, refusing to fight until fired upon. It made him sick.

"Hey, here's Sabinal!" Steck said, seeing the regulator approach.

"Thank God you're all right," Correen said. "We heard shootin'."

Claude got down and motioned for her to take his mount.

"What happened?" Bob asked.

"It was the one they called Squaw Man. We had a runnin' fight and he got to ridin' so hard in the dark that he rimrocked himself. Rode right off the bluff where all those dead sheep were. Killed him deader than hell."

"That's one less outlaw to worry about," Steck said.

"And eight more to take his place," Claude replied. "I spotted Ike's bunch this mornin'. About a mile away when I saw 'em, and ridin' this way. They probably heard the shootin' last night, too. They'll be on my trail by now."

"Eight riders?" Lone Wolf said. "They'll have good horses, and us with these mustangs. Maybe we'd better make a run for Laramie."

Claude had been waiting for this. "And guard our hind ends all the way there? Hell, no. You've got to feel some grit, Wolverton. Right now they don't know we're mounted, so it's the best time to attack. See if we can't even the odds some."

Wolverton shook his head. "I think we should go back to Laramie and get some kind of legal authority before we start killin' any more men."

"I've got legal authority," Steck said. "I'm a reserve deputy sheriff back home."

Claude mounted the bay mare and sighed as if in disgust. "Dammit, Wolverton, they've killed Little Crow and shot at every one of us. They've killed our horses and stolen Bob's cattle. What more do you want?"

"He's right," Correen said. "We've got to attack now while we have the one advantage."

Wolverton's head was still shaking. "If we get more men, we can surround 'em and make 'em surrender. I'll fight when I have to, but till then I'll go out of my way to keep from killin' another man."

"Then you can hold the horses while this old cripple and this little hundred-pound woman does your fightin' for you," Claude said.

"Here now!" Steck said. "No need to get all that familiar, Sabinal. I'm still bankrollin' this outfit."

"No offense, Bob, but that leg of yours don't look good."

"Callin' me cripple don't rile me, but don't you go callin' me old!"

"And don't you go callin' me a coward," Wolverton warned.

Correen moved between the two men. "No one spoke that word."

"No, but he's talkin' all around it," Wolverton said, "and I'm tired of it."

"Hell, I'll say it. I think you're a coward. By God, a man who won't fight when he ought to is a coward."

Wolverton got down from the lead mare and handed his reins to Correen. "Years ago I'd have killed you for sayin' that. Now I'll satisfy myself with just beatin' the tar out of you. Get down."

"Don't mind if I do," Claude said. He gave his

reins to Steck as he hit the ground and let his gun belt drop.

"Stop it!" Correen ordered.

But Claude was already in motion, running toward the big man. Wolverton came ahead, too, and they rushed together like two fighting bulls, even to the point that they butted heads, knocking each other's hats off. Each grabbed with one hand and punched with the other. Claude lost his footing and fell, but pulled Wolverton down with him, and they rolled like schoolboys in the dirt.

"Get up!" Correen shouted. "Stop that!"

Wolverton tried to pin Claude, but the regulator swung a knee into the big man's ribs and they rolled far enough apart to get back on their feet.

Correen got down from Casino and handed Steck the reins of the lead mare, the old rancher absorbed in the fight, hardly noticing her.

The brawlers panted and circled for a few seconds, until Claude rushed Lone Wolf again. They traded a few solid punches, the toes of their boots inches apart, until Correen came between them with a pine stick. "Stop it!" she said, hitting Claude over the left shoulder. The regulator staggered back as the stick broke over Wolverton's forehead.

"Whoa," Steck said, holding the two skittish mounts.

Correen cleared the air between the two men with what was left of her stick. "Stop behavin' so stupid! We've got eight killers almost upon us, and all you can think of is fightin' each other!"

Claude took his mustang from Steck, stepped

up on the stirrup. She was right, of course, but he had taunted Wolverton with purpose. For one thing, it had felt good to release some of his old anger. For another, he thought maybe he had gotten Wolverton into a fighting mood.

The big man rubbed his head, spit blood, took the reins of the lead mare from Steck.

The rancher chuckled. "You're gonna have to let 'em get it out of their craw sooner or later, Correen. I don't care if you break a whole forest of sticks over their head, them boys are gonna fight. Probably make best friends once they get it over with."

Claude reined south. "My best friend's dead."

Thirty-two

~o~

Giff Dearborn lay on his back, balancing his foot on a spur rowel, a roll of blankets under his head. The smell of frying bacon drifted under his nose as he drummed his fingers against the canteen on his chest.

"Let me go over it one more time," he said. "You got this character, Claude Duval, in charge. Good tracker, good with a gun."

"Right," Lafferty said, a curl of wood dropping from his whittling stick. "If he's good enough to run Squaw Man off the mountain, he's damn good."

"Then there's Wolverton. Got the Creedmoor now, but he's turned preacher and won't fight unless he has to."

"That's the way it looks. He could have picked us off anytime at Wild Roy's hideout, but he waited till the last possible second. Didn't he, Clay?"

Sickle nodded his drooping head. He sat against a big deadfall, a blanket over his shoulders, his face pale as snow.

"And Duval don't get along with Wolverton," Dearborn continued. "That could work in our favor." He adjusted his hat around the curl on his crown. "Then there's the feisty old bastard from Texas, and the crack-shot woman."

"Crack shot is right," Lafferty said. "And she don't panic under fire."

"And one horse among 'em." Dearborn inhaled the aroma of biscuits, rolling his eyes to one side to see how far along the cook was with lunch. He swept his eyes around the circle of gunmen. They weren't professionals, but they had all done a little shooting. His hunch was that not all of them would be riding out of these mountains. "This ought to be easy enough," he said.

The coffeepot rang suddenly like a bell as two holes appeared in it, one circled by curled points of torn metal. It swung violently over the fire, issuing two streams that hissed on hot coals, going up in steam. The gunmen flinched, the rifle blast still ringing in their ears.

"Don't move!" a voice said from the timber. "Give up, Ike, or we'll shoot in there among you."

Dearborn shot a look at Lafferty, drew his Colt, rolled to the big deadfall for cover, and fired toward the voice in the timber. Lafferty rolled in beside him.

The cook reached for a rifle but fell with a bullet hole in his chest. Three points of fire opened up, all on the north side of camp. Sickle fell over on his side, caressing a rifle but feeling too weak to use it.

Two cowboys fell, one screaming in pain. Others scattered, looking for cover, firing blindly.

Dearborn stuck his head up, fired four quick rounds, glimpsed a woman retreating up the slope and over the rise. "Get the horses!" he shouted, jumping to his feet. "Run 'em down!"

Ike Lafferty rose calmly beside him and took off his hat. He put his finger through a hole in the side of the crown. "That one parted my hair," he said, walking with Dearborn to the horses.

"Yeah, crosswise," Dearborn replied. "Wonder what they've got planned. They shouldn't be harassin' us like that."

Lafferty glanced back at the two dying men on the ground. "Maybe they're just tryin' to draw us out where Wolverton can get a bead on us. I haven't heard that Creedmoor fire yet."

Dearborn pulled himself up by the saddle horn as he grabbed his reins. "He can't shoot us all with a single-shot rifle."

"Dammit," Lafferty said, looking back over the camp before riding out. "They got my cook. Now the grub's gonna burn."

They put spurs to their mounts and rode for the rise where Dearborn had seen the woman disappear. The cowboys in front of them stopped at the ridge, staring down at the terrain below.

"Emmett, what are you waitin' for?" Lafferty asked as he rode up beside his foreman. He expected to see the three attackers on foot down below, but found nothing.

"Where the hell did they go?" Dearborn said.

Along a trail on the next ridge, they glimpsed two riders passing a gap in the trees, neither riding the big paint they had expected.

"Son of a bitch," Lafferty said. "They got horses somewhere."

"Now what are we gonna do?" Emmett said.

Dearborn lifted his hat, briefly twisting the scalp lock on his crown. "You all stay behind 'em, but don't press 'em too hard," he replied. "Give me a chance to get around in front of 'em."

"What are you gonna do?" Lafferty asked.

"Hell, I don't know. I ain't there yet." He spurred his mount down from the rise and left the other riders behind, his stirrups slapping against the flanks of his mount as he plunged down the grassy slope.

"I guess we hit four of 'em hard enough to keep 'em out of the saddle," Claude said, watching the gang lope toward him. "Could have got five if you'd have done more than hold the horses."

Wolverton ignored the taunt, his eyes sweeping the parks and ridges for more riders. "Did you give 'em a chance to surrender?"

"I'm sure we did," Correen said. "But we didn't expect they would."

"Maybe they will now, the odds bein' even."

"They don't look like they're surrenderin' to me," Steck said. "Looks like they're comin' for a fight."

"Wonder why they're comin' so slow," Wolverton said. "You sure you got four? They may have split up."

"They ain't splittin' up, they're just comin' to kill us," Claude said. "You remember that big park west of here?"

Lone Wolf nodded.

"You and Creedmoor go get ready on the west side of it. We'll see if we can draw 'em out in the open after us, and you can pick Lafferty off."

Wolverton sat silent in the saddle.

"Well, git!" Claude ordered.

The big man frowned and turned his worried eyes to Correen. Only when she nodded would he touch his spurs to the lead mare. Claude ground his teeth and felt a vast distance between Correen and himself. Not the kind of thing he wanted to worry about now. When this business was over, maybe he could show her how much of a gentleman he could be when he wasn't hunting outlaws. Then again, maybe it would be too late.

Dearborn leaped from the saddle and loosened the cinch as the pony stood heaving. He let his reins drop and scrambled up the slope. Approaching the rise, he threw his hat down, dropped to his stomach, and slithered ahead. He could hear his mount puffing behind him as he peeked over the ridge.

A single rider caught his eye. A big man on a big bay horse, far off, riding hard across a wide park. Had to be Wolverton. A flash of white drew his attention to the east. He made out the paint stallion, the woman perched on top like a child. She was riding just behind two men head-reining their horses. They must have come across some green-broke stock somewhere. Searching farther east, he saw Ike and his boys loping over a rise, stopping to look at the sign on the ground.

Looking back to the west, he saw Wolverton dismount at the far edge of the park, a long rifle in his hand—a mere toothpick from this distance. Was the old assassin going to fight? Looked that way. Lying down on his stomach now, preparing to shoot.

Dearborn scooted back from the ridge, grabbed his hat, and ran back down to his mount. In a few seconds he had tightened the girth and was on his way, still not sure what he was going to do. All he really wanted was Wolverton's scalp. This idea of running Ike's rustling gang wasn't altogether unattractive, but it wasn't what he had come here for.

He circled, keeping high ground between himself and the other riders. He had to get closer if he was going to make something happen. He would figure out what to do when the time came. That was the way he liked it, anyway.

A hard push got him to the big park somewhere between Wolverton and the other three vigilantes. He stayed back in the timber, not anxious to let Lone Wolf find him in the sights of the Creedmoor. He found a heavily timbered draw at the lower end of the park and stayed in its cover, watching and listening for opportunities.

He had been sneaking through the brush long enough to let his pony catch some wind when he heard the approach of the horses. Through the oak leaves he saw Duval, the gray-haired rancher, and the woman on the big paint. Duval searched the park and pointed toward Wolverton at the far side. They looked over their shoulders for pursuers, then angled toward the head of Dearborn's wooded draw.

Dearborn guessed what they were doing. Luring Lafferty and his men into the open where Wolverton could pick them off with the Creedmoor. Yet, they were playing it safe, staying close to cover, skirting the edge of the park. In fact, it looked as though they would come right by the heavy timber of the draw Dearborn was hiding in.

He drew his revolver and moved his pony step by step, closer to the sunlit openness of the park. As long as they were moving, they probably wouldn't see him coming through the shadows. It was time to make something happen.

He caught it like a spark. The woman was the key. The bargaining chip. He could get whatever he wanted out of this expedition through her. She was riding in the rear still, two or three lengths behind the men, the big paint she rode prancing like a wild stallion herding his harem. Dearborn could hear their saddles squeak.

"Come on," Duval growled, trying to wrench his mustang's head away from the timber. The claybank Steck rode proved no more cooperative, and the riders found little opportunity to watch for enemies.

Dearborn remained motionless, let them pass the draw. Then he came out silently, at a walk, trailing Correen. Once in the open, he spurred his horse hard and rode for the woman.

Casino sensed the attack first, craning his neck to see behind. Correen gasped as she reached for the Winchester in her saddle scabbard. "Claude!" she shouted.

Dearborn let loose a Comanche yell as he closed the gap between himself and the woman. The green-broke horses lunged against every effort to turn them. The woman had the Winchester out, but Dearborn was there, springing from his saddle, landing right behind Correen on the big prancing paint. He wrenched the Winchester away and dropped it. He put his hand around her tiny fist, mastering the reins. The muzzle of his pistol felt cold under her chin.

Claude was on the ground, drawing a pistol, holding a rein. But it was too late. The stranger had Correen, had Casino, had control.

"I love ridin' double with a pretty woman!" Dearborn shouted. "Turn loose of that pistol, and she'll be all right."

"Turn loose of her, or you won't!" Claude warned.

"Can't do that! Once you get aholt of a wildcat, you'd better keep a firm grip!" His maniacal laughter ripped across the park like a donkey's bray.

Steck had his claybank turned around and was heading back toward Dearborn. "You'd better not harm her!" the old rancher shouted.

Dearborn rode Casino in front of his mount, herding the riderless pony toward timber. "She'll be all right. Y'all just stay put here and I'll be back directly—let you know what it'll cost you to get her back."

Claude thought about chancing a shot as Dearborn rode broadside into cover. Correen's eyes told him to do it, but he couldn't with the pistol barrel at her throat.

As she disappeared, he felt a pang in his

chest. Little things she had said to him over the past few days came unexplainably to mind:

"Your sideburns are lopsided ... Sacred cattle in the sacred mountains ... Thank God you're all right."

And even his own name in her lovely Old World voice. Yes, just now. She had called him by his Christian name. Before she could think, she had called it out: "Claude!" And he had done nothing.

Thirty-three

꘎ꝏ꘎

Duval!"

The voice knifed through the trees, a shrill cry reaching Claude's ears.

"I know you're out there! Let's talk!"

He got up and showed himself to the man who had taken Correen.

He had followed the kidnapper to Ike's camp, ordering Steck and Wolverton to stay back unless they heard gunfire. He had watched the camp for an hour as Ike's men planned their strategy and guarded Correen. Now the shadows were long, the cold night coming on. But at least something was happening.

The stranger left the tents behind and approached him, weaving his way among the trembling aspens, armed with a single revolver in his gun belt. He was smiling. As he walked up to Claude he stuck out his hand, as if he wanted to shake. "Howdy," he said.

Claude looked disdainfully at the callus-armored grip. "What do you want?"

"You don't remember me, do you?" He spoke low, his voice falling short of the camp.

"Should I?"

"We stood in the same courtroom eleven years ago. I'm Giff Dearborn."

The regulator's eyes shifted. He remembered now: the outlaw showing up at Lone Wolf's sentencing. Someone next to him had elbowed him and said, "That's Giff Dearborn. That's the feller Lone Wolf thought he was killin' when he shot that poor cowboy."

He looked the man over from spurs to hat.

"You remember now?"

Claude remembered plenty. Would any of this be happening if Wolverton had killed the right man eleven years ago? He hated this: dealing with Dearborn for Correen's life. Dearborn was no better than Wolverton, maybe lower. "You had gall showin' up in a court of law," he said.

Dearborn laughed as if having the time of his life. "Hell, wasn't no gall about it. The law didn't have a damn thing on me. Why do you think them ranchers wanted me Lone-Wolfed?"

The regulator scratched his beard. "What are you doin' up here in this country?"

"Same as you. Came to kill Lone Wolf. It's riled me for years, thinkin' he'd back-shoot me."

"If that's all you wanted, why'd you throw in with Lafferty? Why'd you take the girl?"

Dearborn set his sweatband back behind the tuft on his head and twisted the curl. "Seemed like a good idea at the time. Thought I'd take over the Snowy Range Gang, but now I've changed my mind. Gettin' too dangerous." He flashed a smile. "I'm willin' to give the girl back."

"What about Lafferty?"

"I don't give a damn for Lafferty. All I want is Lone Wolf. You and Steck and the girl can go your own way as far as I'm concerned."

Claude shifted his weight to his other foot, tucked his thumbs under his gun belt. "What do you have in mind?"

Dearborn grinned. "Simple. I'll swap you the girl for a clean shot at Lone Wolf."

Claude stared, no expression on his face. "There's not a damn simple thing about it. What about Ike and his boys with all those complications strapped around their hips?"

Dearborn nodded. "I've been thinkin' about that." He crossed his arms over his chest. "How's this: Let's tell Ike you killed Lone Wolf."

"What the hell for?"

"Ike knows you want Lone Wolf dead, and he hasn't seen the big bastard since you all had that scrape at the outlaw camp. If Ike thinks it's just you and Steck, he'll get overconfident. He'll think it's us five outlaws against you two regulators."

"The truth is, it's you five outlaws against us three regulators. And you have Correen. I still don't like the odds."

"Goddamn, Duval, you're missin' the mark. I'm comin' over to your side. Loyalty never was one of my stronger points, anyway." He jabbed a trigger finger at the Texan, leered with a ridiculous face. "It'll be me, you, Steck, and Wolverton against Ike and his three boys. Four against four. But we'll have the surprise on 'em. Anyway, that one redheaded feller's got the grippe so bad he won't be no good for nothin'."

"And nobody will be shootin' at you, because everybody thinks you're on their side."

Dearborn smirked at the sky. "By God, I hadn't thought of that!"

Claude was mulling the deal over from every angle. "So you want to beat Ike out of the girl, then you want to turn on Wolverton and kill him?"

"Don't you?"

Claude didn't like it. He didn't like a man who changed sides in the middle of a fight. He didn't like selling somebody out—not even Wolverton. The only thing he did like was the glimmer of hope this conniving Giff Dearborn had brought. Hope that he would see Correen alive again. He forced his cracked lips into a smile. "I like it," he said.

Dearborn scraped some ground bare with his boot and squatted on his heels. He urged Claude to hunker down beside him and began drawing a rough map in the dirt. "Here's how Ike wants to do it. There's a bare pass in the divide south of here . . ."

"Well?" Steck said when Claude came back to their hideout in the timber. "What do they want?"

Claude pulled his knife from his pocket and unfolded a blade he had filed square at the end. He picked up his Marlin rifle and began removing a screw holding the rawhide-wrapped stock to the gun. "We may have a chance. One of Ike's boys says he wants to turn on Ike and help us get Correen back."

"Bullshit," Steck said. "You believe that?"

"I think he means it. Says he doesn't want any part of killin' a woman."

"Sounds like bait to me," Steck said.

"You know Correen," Claude said. "She could charm a snake into bitin' itself. She's already got this outlaw halter broke and leadin'."

Steck put his hand on his chin and raised an eyebrow. "Well, now, that does sound like Correen. What's he gonna do? Sneak her over to us tonight?"

"I suggested that. Too risky for him. He wants us to take all the chances while he guards his hind end."

"What do we do?" Wolverton asked.

Claude glowered at the big man in the dying light. "Are you ready to shoot now?"

"Yes."

"You'd better hope it's not too late." He threw the stock of the Marlin aside and started unscrewing the barrel band to remove the forestock. "Now, to make this work, Bob, your leg's got to be busted. And, Wolverton, you've got to be dead ..."

Thirty-four

❧

They found the place in the moon-light—a treeless, saddle-shaped pass in the Medicine Bow Divide. By the time they crawled into position on the high northern rim, the moon had sunk beyond the Park Range, draining the mountains of light. They hid between clumps of wind-twisted evergreens, staring silently down at the pass, barely visible in the starlight.

"I see why Ike picked this place," Claude said, his words trailing away on a cold breeze. "Must be a mile across with no cover. That makes for a long ambush, even for you and the Creedmoor."

"I thought Ike was supposed to think I'm dead."

"He's supposed to, but that doesn't mean he does."

Wolverton grunted and they looked down at the windswept saddle in silence.

"Ike will come up the east slope with Correen and all his boys," Claude finally said, pointing. "Me and Bob will come up from the west. My guess is they'll try to talk us out of our guns first. When we refuse, Ike will probably have some signal planned for his boys to start shootin'. He'll have Correen shieldin' him, so his boys will be takin' all the chances. He won't know about you up here, though. With any luck, you'll get to take your shot first."

"How's your hand?" Lone Wolf asked. "That sore's not gonna slow you down, is it?"

Claude flexed the bandaged hand. The swelling was down, the pain hardly noticeable. He had to admit, the wild lettuce seemed to have helped. "You worry about your own shots. How far away you reckon the bottom of that saddle is?"

"Hard to tell in the dark. I'd say close to seven hundred yards."

Claude shook his head and sighed. "You ever shot that far?"

"I've shot targets at a thousand yards."

"How long was the farthest shot you ever took at a man?"

"A little over six hundred," the big man muttered.

Claude whistled under his breath. "Hit him?"

"Killed him."

"Who was it?"

Lone Wolf stared blankly down at the saddle, the Creedmoor lying in his open palms. His silence gripped Claude like a stranglehold as a quarter mile of wind whipped between them.

Everything kept coming back to Dusty. He couldn't forget if he wanted to. And he *didn't* want to. In fact, he was scared senseless that someday he'd forget. What kind of man would that make him, if he failed to keep that promise he had spoken to his dead partner the day he found Dusty facedown in his own campfire?

He wished he had never gotten to know Wolverton. It would have been easy killing him as a stranger. He still didn't like the man but had found qualities there he had never expected.

He thought about Giff Dearborn's deal. "You should have stayed in Texas, Lone Wolf. You know what I have to do if I make it past tomorrow alive."

"I know what you think you have to do. I even understand it. Used to think along those lines myself. I just hope you change your mind when the time comes."

Claude scoffed into the wind. "I can't wait to haul off and kick your carcass and see that you don't even flinch. Dreamed of it for years. Maybe you think you've paid for killin' my partner, but I just see one way you can pay. I don't care that you made a mistake, either. There's some things you just can't let go as accidents."

"It wasn't an accident."

"What?" Claude growled.

"It was God's will. If it hadn't been for Dusty, I'd still be murderin' now."

Claude's muscles writhed, his hands gathering fists full of gravel. "What the hell do you know about God's will, you back-shootin' son of a bitch?"

Lone Wolf took his hat off and looked at the stars around him. Here, on this high, barren ridge, he felt as if among them—one shining soul in a flock. The Milky Way coursed lazily down upon him, bathing him. He rolled onto his back, pillowed his head on his old hat, watched his breath-cloud catch the starlight.

"I believe a star burns for every soul who ever lived," he said. "I believe a life is like a light. Maybe you think you kill it when you snuff it out, but it don't die. It just keeps goin' into space, shootin' quicker than a sound, or a glance, or a bullet. Farther than you can see. Farther than you ever thought things went. Look at 'em up there. Millions of 'em."

Claude looked around in spite of himself, felt the cold night on the back of his neck as his long hair fell away from his skin. A shooting star raked far across the sky, leaving a trail in a quick flash.

"Now, you see that?" Wolverton said. "There went somebody's lifetime spent wasted. That was me before I knew Dusty."

"You *didn't* know Dusty."

"No, not the way you did."

"What the hell does that mean?"

Lone Wolf let the Creedmoor lie across his chest, and put his hands in his coat pockets. "The day after I shot your partner, one of the ranchers who'd hired me asked me why I hadn't killed Giff Dearborn yet. Said he'd seen him in town. I figured out what I'd done then, so I tore out for New Mexico.

"That night I stared up at the sky. Couldn't sleep. And I saw a new star come out right in front of my open eyes, takin' up a patch of dark sky that never saw light before.

"I never looked at Dusty Sanderson's face. Never heard his voice. That night I didn't even know his name. Didn't know yet who I'd killed.

But I knew that was his light, and I knew what I had to do. I started livin' that night."

Claude searched the sky. He felt depth he had never noticed before, distance he had never fathomed, loneliness he knew too well.

"I know Dusty," Wolverton said, "and he won't let me forget. He crosses over every night, straight and steady. He shines true. That's his star way up yonder."

Claude felt the cold air in his windpipe, the solid mountain pressing up under him. The sky all but swallowed him in a spray of light. "What star?" he groaned, as if to ridicule. But he wanted to know that light. It was just like Dusty to come back as such.

The long arm swept slowly upward, a gnarled finger jutting. "There . . ."

Thirty-five

~∞~

Like a smile, the great curve of the saddle appeared against the dawn sky. When the light suited Ike Lafferty, he arrived at the bottom of the curve, his arm wrapped around Correen, holding her as a shield in front of him, his pistol under her ear. Four men appeared beside him.

"Here we go," Claude said. They stepped out of the trees and started up the slope to the divide, Claude on foot, Steck riding the bay mare. "When we get close, stay over to the left," he said. "I don't want to be lookin' right into the sun."

"Our left or their left?" Steck asked.

"Our left, dammit. What do I care about their left?"

Steck chuckled. "Take it easy, Sabinal. I was just needlin' you some to take the edge off."

Claude shot a glance up at him. "Whatever you do, don't look up at Wolverton's position. They'll catch you lookin' and know he's up there."

"Hell, I didn't want to look till you said that."

"Well, don't."

They walked the rest of the way in silence, squinting into the eastern sky. Lafferty stood at the left, pressing Correen against him with more familiarity than Claude could enjoy. Emmett, the ranch foreman, stood next to Lafferty. Then there was the redheaded Sickle twin, looking pale and poorly, shivering visibly. Next, a cowboy called Joe, if Claude remembered the name correctly. And finally, Giff Dearborn at the far right.

A breeze tossed his hair back from his collar when he reached the divide, and Claude wondered what the windage adjustment would be on the Creedmoor for this distance, this wind speed. The Laramie Plains stretched away into a haze far below. He looked each man in the eye as Steck reined in the bay mare. Then he looked at Correen, her big green eyes alert and misty.

"Mornin', Sabinal; Bob," Ike said smugly.

Steck grimaced as he swung a splinted right leg over the saddle and lowered himself from the seat, holding a rein. He took a couple of hops away from the horse, stretched his right leg out in front of him, and sat awkwardly on the cold ground. The leg had two pine boughs lashed to it with rawhide. He rubbed his knee tenderly as he looked up at the outlaws, resisting a glance at Lone Wolf's position on the high ridge to the left.

"That leg botherin' you where you fell off the bluff?" Ike said.

"I didn't fall, I jumped," Steck replied. "And it wasn't the jump that busted it, it was you bastards shootin' my horse dead in the creek." He lifted the splinted leg from the ground as he rubbed it.

"What do you hold it up like that for?" Emmett said.

"Because it don't hurt so much when I do, stupid." He pointed his boot heel at a gap between two of the men and massaged his knee.

"Let's get down to business," Claude said. "Let the girl go and give her ten minutes' head start on the horse, then the rest of us will decide how to finish this thing off."

Lafferty glanced down the line of men at Dearborn. "Is that what you told him we were gonna do, Giff?"

"Wasn't that the plan?" Giff said, smiling and shrugging.

"I'm afraid there's been a little mix-up, Sabinal. I ain't about to turn loose of this woman until you and Steck lay your guns down."

Steck lowered his splinted leg gingerly to the ground and lay back on his elbows.

Claude shook his head. "The odds are against me bad enough as it is, Ike. You've got five men against two."

"Five against three, for all I know. Wolverton could be out there with that old Sharps."

"He's dead."

Correen suddenly kicked a spray of rocks at Claude, causing every man but Sickle to flinch. "You fool!" she said, her voice a savage growl. "Did you have to tell them you'd killed him?"

Claude quickly caught her drift. "Oh, shut up,

Correen. It don't do no good to bluff like he's out there if he ain't."

Ike chuckled. "It hasn't been a real pleasant couple of days in camp for you all, has it?"

Steck elevated his leg and rubbed his knee again.

"We had an agreement," Claude said. "Let the woman go, like we decided."

Lafferty shook his head. "I'm still not convinced about Wolverton. If he's dead, where's the Creedmoor?"

"Busted," Bob said, lowering his splints. "Sabinal used it to cave in Lone Wolf's skull, and just kept beatin' his brains out till he'd busted that skinny little stock off that rifle and boogered the block all up. Then he just threw it out in the woods somewhere."

Lafferty studied Steck's face, then looked at Claude. "If you wanted to kill him, why didn't you just shoot him?"

"I didn't want to advertise where we were. You had that black man huntin' us."

Ike grunted. "You believe 'em, Giff?"

Dearborn crossed his arms over his chest and cocked his head to one side. "I believe if I was them, I'd be lyin' my ass off about now. But I ain't seen no sign of Wolverton, and we are way out here away from cover."

"You want proof he's dead?" Claude asked. "I got it in my saddlebag." He stepped toward the horse.

"Careful," Lafferty warned. "Last time you reached into that saddlebag you pulled out a pistol."

"No, you be careful," Claude said, raking the men with his eyes. "Any of your boys touches a gun butt and all hell's gonna break loose." He unbuckled the saddlebag flap with one hand, watching the men. He reached inside and slowly withdrew a patch of black hair.

"What's that supposed to be?" Lafferty said.

"It's what's left of Lone Wolf's scalp," Bob replied.

"Oh, son of a bitch," Emmett groaned, his lip curling.

"Let me see it," Ike ordered.

Claude took a few steps toward Lafferty, then stopped, and tossed the scalp toward the outlaw boss, landing it at Correen's feet.

"Darlin'," Ike said, keeping his eyes riveted to Duval, "bend over and pick that up, will you?"

The right side of Correen's mouth smiled at Claude, where only he could see, and she bent slowly to pick up the tuft of hair, her own trusses falling around it as she reached. For an instant, the barrel of Ike's revolver angled away from her head.

Claude saw the wind tear a stream of black smoke away from the ridge to his left, high and far away, out of focus. Time slowed, like molasses through an hourglass. To his right, he sensed Bob's splinted leg rising and knew the old rancher had seen the muzzle blast of the Creedmoor, too.

Sickle started to say something.

The regulator concentrated on what he had to do. When the big slug from the Sharps hit Lafferty, he would draw a Russian to gun down the man next to Ike—the ranch foreman called Emmett. Bob would take the Sickle boy. Giff Dearborn would turn on the man at his side— the cowboy called Joe.

Sickle's words had arrived slow as a bayou: "They scalped that squaw."

The slug popped against Ike Lafferty's shoulder, whipping his head back as his chest spewed blood. He fell on top of Correen as Claude reached toward his holster and the green mare broke to run down the mountain.

Steck pointed his boot heel at Sickle and reached into a slit in his pants leg. He pulled the trigger of the Marlin rifle, stripped of butt and forestock, lashed to his leg under the fabric of his trousers. The bullet tore through boot leather at his ankle and hit Sickle high in the stomach, folding him back like a cellar door slamming shut on a freight hole.

Claude had Emmett covered before the foreman could get his grip around his pistol, but something was wrong. Dearborn was standing, waiting. Cowboy Joe was drawing a side arm. Steck was trying to get his Colt out of his holster.

Claude saw the fear in Emmett's eyes when he fired, spinning the foreman. He thumbed the hammer as he turned.

Cowboy Joe shot down at Bob Steck, and now, too late, Giff Dearborn drew a weapon and fired at the man beside him, as Claude did the same, catching the cowboy in a cross fire that doubled him over and rolled him down the mountain slope.

Dearborn looked back at Duval to find the big Smith & Wesson staring him in the face. He waited for the sounds of the runaway horse and the echoing gunshots to die.

"He was fast with that pistol," Dearborn said. "Faster than I thought." He let his Colt slip into its holster and pitched his hat back on his head, feeling for the curl of his scalp lock.

"He wasn't fast," Claude said, stalking toward the outlaw. "You were slow. You waited, you son of a bitch." He brought the barrel of his .44 down on the twisted curl atop Dearborn's head. The outlaw collapsed.

Turning, he saw Correen crawling out from under Ike's limp body. He followed her eyes to Bob Steck, saw the old Texan holding back a current of blood streaming from his vest. He knelt to one side of Steck as Correen came to the other.

"Hang on, Bob. We'll get you out of here and take a look at that wound."

Steck shook his head. "Don't waste your strength. I'm hit too bad."

Correen put her thigh under Steck's head like a pillow.

He smiled up at her, then looked at Claude. "Send them bremmers back to Texas, Sabinal, but keep a couple of bulls for yourself. I left instructions to get you paid, in case I didn't come back." He grinned. "And it don't look like I'm goin' back."

Claude caught a glimpse of motion and glanced up to find Wolverton running down into the saddle, still a few hundred yards away.

Steck lifted his head to look at his wound. "Lone Wolf made a hell of a shot on Ike, didn't he? I didn't want to say it, Sabinal, and crush what little morale we had, but I didn't think he could make that shot." He let his head sink back to Correen's thigh as she stroked his white hair back over his head. "What are you gonna do about Lone Wolf? You gonna let him go back to Texas?"

Claude looked over his shoulder to check on Dearborn. "I don't know."

Correen looked across the dying man and stared in astonishment at the regulator.

"Well, anyway," Steck said, heaving now, his eyelids sinking, "it ain't my worry. You'll do what's right. Your folks down in Texas ought to be proud of you." His eyes closed, and his bloody hand slid to the ground. "Have Lone Wolf say a few words over me." He smiled. "Thank God I ain't dyin' in no rockin' chair."

Claude stared down at Steck until he realized the life had left him. He could hear Wolverton's footsteps now, rattling rocks as the big man trotted toward the bloody ground of the fight.

Correen slipped her leg out from under Steck's head. She ran to meet Wolverton over the body of Ike Lafferty. Claude felt the morning chill when he saw her embrace the big man, pressing her face against his chest as she wrapped her arms around him. He had never felt such a helpless jealous rage.

He turned away and looked down the slope to the west, where the mustang had disappeared. He squinted, blinked. There they were again. Standing in a line, staring at him, their humps listing. Sacred cattle in the sacred mountains.

Thirty-six

⁓

The broad flat neck of the claybank felt warm where the strong sunlight struck her. Claude patted her as he led her to the mound of dirt Correen and Lone Wolf were smoothing.

They had chosen an open park with a good view west to bury Bob Steck. Wolverton had fashioned a cross of pine boughs and set it deep at the head of the grave.

"Ol' Bob can see the Great Divide from here," Claude said, his voice expressionless. He slipped Steck's Winchester into its scabbard.

Correen looked up from the grave and saw the claybank wearing Steck's saddle, rope, bedroll. "Mr. Duval, what on earth . . ."

Wolverton silenced her with a touch on the shoulder.

Claude turned the mare to the west, looking out over the slope of the park. "I cut almost all the way through the cinch. She'll bust it in a few days and shake the saddle off. If she's lucky, she'll never wear one again."

The wild mare rolled her eyes nervously as Claude worked his hand toward her head. "Well, ol' girl, you're carryin' everything he'll need. A good rifle and a stout rope." He put his hand on the headstall, and the mare flinched, jumping aside. "Whoa, now, it ain't so bad. If you were a Indian horse, we'd shoot you and leave you lay on the grave."

He worked his hand under the bridle and pulled it off. The mare jerked her head back, then stood confused, unsure of her freedom.

"Go on!" Claude shouted. "Git!" He lashed the claybank's rump with the reins of Steck's bridle. The mare bolted, ran halfway across the park, then started pitching. "Run, you knothead!" the regulator shouted. He dropped the bridle and pulled both Russians from his holsters, firing them alternately in the air until the mustang had run for the timber, her head and tail high, mane streaming over the empty saddle.

"Now, that's a cowboy funeral," Claude said, the echoes of gunfire sounding like thunder from his throat. "Would have suited Bob." He picked up the bridle and left it hanging on the pine cross as he hiked uphill for the horses.

Correen and Lone Wolf looked uncertainly at each other, wondering what Claude had in mind next. They followed him up the mountainside.

Giff Dearborn was sitting against a tree, his hands tied in front of him, his neck leashed to the trunk. A streak of dried blood—cracked like parched soil—ran from his scalp lock, between his eyes, down one side of his nose. It jumped his mouth and disappeared under his chin. He had a fierce headache, and his stomach was fighting pangs of nausea.

"Hey, Duval," he said as the three regulators began shaping up their midday camp. "What about our deal?"

"I don't hold to deals with horse thieves," he said, stroking Casino. "Anyway, you didn't keep your end."

"What deal?" Correen asked.

Claude glanced at her, but he was still reeling with envy over the way she had embraced Wolverton, and he couldn't look her in the eye. "Ol' Giff here sold out on Ike. He was supposed to help us get you back in exchange for me givin' him a shot at Wolverton. But when it came time to shoot it out with Ike's bunch, he waited to see who would win the fight. He knew nobody would be shootin' at him. He waited, and got Bob killed."

Correen tried to get in front of Claude, but he turned away. "You weren't really going to let this man shoot Mr. Wolverton?"

"If anybody's gonna shoot Mr. Wolverton, it's gonna be me."

"Hell, I don't care who shoots him, long as I get to see it!" Dearborn said.

"Shut up," Claude warned.

"Duval!" Lone Wolf's voice said, barking across the camp. He was pulling the long barrel of the Creedmoor from his saddle boot. "I'm tired of all this talk. If you're gonna kill me, you're gonna do it before we leave this camp."

"Don't tempt me," Claude said.

"That's exactly what I intend to do." He

pitched the rifle at the regulator. "You can use this and add it to your collection."

Claude caught the gun, tossed it back. "You're the one knows how to shoot it."

Wolverton frowned at the Creedmoor, threw it back at Claude, putting his muscle behind it this time. "I don't want it," he growled.

Claude enjoyed seeing the big man flustered, felt an urge to taunt him. "Why not? It fired true enough for you this mornin'. What's wrong with it?"

"The serial number."

"Huh?" Claude rolled the Creedmoor onto its back and looked at the number stamped on the belly. "What's wrong with it? Not low enough for you?"

"That's not just any Sharps Creedmoor. That's my old gun. That's the gun I killed Dusty with."

"Oh, I'd shoot the son of a bitch now for sure," Dearborn said.

Correen stepped in front of Wolverton, as if to shield him, though he looked twice as tall as she. "You're not going to do any more killin', Mr. Duval."

Wolverton moved her aside with a long arm. "Get out of the way, Correen. I have to get this over with."

Claude swung the Creedmoor around on Wolverton. "You want it over with? I can oblige you." The gun in his hands made him think of the moment he had visualized in a thousand nightmares: the long rifle kicking, Dusty falling, Wolverton pressing the cartridge into his dead partner's hand, the smell of burning flesh in the air.

"I tried to explain it to you last night," Lone Wolf said, standing tall, legs apart, the Snowy

Range over his shoulder. "Dusty means somethin' good to me. To you he's just a reason to kill. You call Dusty your partner, but since I killed him, he's been closer to me than he has been to you. Dusty's *my* partner now. He don't ride with you anymore."

Claude vaguely heard his own jaw teeth grinding. The mountains darkened, and he saw only Wolverton, standing in a half-light. He thumbed back the hammer of the Creedmoor. "You want to die, don't you?"

"No," the big man said. "I want to live. But I don't mean walkin' this earth with a dead soul rottin' inside me. If I'm gonna live, I have to get this behind me for good. I've got to have your forgiveness, Sabinal. Otherwise, I might as well be dead."

Claude raised the rifle to his shoulder and stared at the big man through the hooded front sight. "How 'bout if I send my forgiveness right down this long barrel?" His finger wrapped around the trigger.

"It doesn't help," Correen said, her voice calm, like an angel's. "It doesn't make you feel one wee bit better."

"Hell, kill him!" Dearborn said, kicking his boots in the dirt. "The goddamn son of a bitch shot your partner! Shot him in the back and left him lay in the fire!"

"Don't do it," Correen said.

"Kill him, goddammit! Kill him, kill him, kill him!"

The half-light faded around Wolverton, and Claude remembered the horror of rolling Dusty from the fire—flesh burned to the bone; cooked, blackened, blistered; the gaping death smile of Dusty's skull. His finger felt the spring behind the trigger.

Then he blinked, and during the instant of darkness, he began to see it. First the left eyebrow, peaked like a mountaintop. Then the eyes, green like Correen's. Dirty blond hair hat-flattened to Dusty's white brow. A crooked nose, broken that time in Abilene. The high cheeks, sun-browned. The jaw, sharp like a plowshare. And the right corner of Dusty's mouth, curving in perpetual smile . . .

Where you been? he thought, as if his partner had come in late from hunting strays.

"Don't do it, Claude. It ain't worth it. It was supposed to happen this way. Go home, Sabinal. Go on home."

The white mountain sun and the cold fresh air burst upon him, and he heard Giff Dearborn's hellish voice growling:

"Kill him, goddammit! Kill the son of a bitch now!"

Claude swung the long barrel around like a boom, stopping the muzzle between Dearborn's eyes. "If I do any more killin' today, I'm gonna start with you."

Dearborn quaked like an aspen before the wind god, his mouth stuck open.

Claude wheeled, aimed into the sun, and pulled the trigger. The hammer fell on an empty chamber, and only clicked. He looked at Wolverton, and the big man smiled—a friendly smile, almost an apology.

It was a fine acquisition. A collector's item. A showpiece, like the Le Mat grapeshot revolver. The Sharps long-range Creedmoor rifle, Model 73. It would be rare someday.

Claude flipped it in midair, caught the barrel behind the hooded sight. He swung like a lumberjack, cracking the hardwood stock off on the tree trunk above Dearborn's head. Overhanded, splitting stovewood. One-handed, like an ape with a stick, spooking the horses. Like a mad farmer with a hoe, a section worker driving spikes.

The trigger guard rang, glinting sunlight as it flipped away. The breech shot a spark from a boulder. The forestock cracked like a walnut. The long steel barrel sailed away, end over end, above Bob Steck's grave, landing in the middle of the park.

Claude panted for a while, then turned to Lone Wolf. "You're not worth it. Probably just end up back in prison, anyway." He drew his knife, cut Dearborn's leash, and pulled the outlaw to his feet.

"Maybe I will," Wolverton said. "For plowin' too deep, or singin' too loud in church."

Claude led Dearborn to one of the captured mounts. "Get on," he said, virtually lifting the outlaw into the saddle. He mounted Casino and started his prisoner up the slope.

"Where are you goin'?" Correen demanded.

"Takin' this outlaw to Laramie. I'm sure he's wanted somewhere for somethin'."

"Don't you want some help guardin' him?" Wolverton said.

"Hell, no."

"What about the bremmers?" Lone Wolf shouted after the riders in the timber.

"I'll come back for 'em. Don't worry, I'll see that you both get your share of the reward money."

"Aren't you going to say goodbye?" Correen pleaded, her fine voice romping through the forest like frisking squirrels. But she heard only hoofbeats in reply.

Thirty-seven

Claude's boot plowed through the cold ashes until it thumped against a chunk of something solid. Stooping, he picked up a discolored rifle barrel, studied the breech. It looked like the remnants of his old Henry repeater. The fire had destroyed his entire collection, hidden under the floor planks of his frame house. The only piece he had left that was worth anything was the Le Mat grapeshot revolver.

Ike's boys had come calling while he had been away hunting the Snowy Range Gang. They had torched his new house, his shed, his corral. He would be hard-pressed to rebuild before winter.

He tossed the ruined rifle aside as a gust enveloped him in a swirl of dust and ashes.

It didn't really matter. Nothing seemed to matter anymore. He looked back at Casino, standing sleepy-eyed beside a small ponderosa pine, a bremmer bull to either side of him. The big paint looked gaunt from his ordeal in the Medicine Bows, but now he would have time to rest and put some fat on before winter.

Claude had a good deal of money coming: rewards from Bob Steck's family and the state of Colorado. He had the two bremmer bulls to start a breeding program with. He still had his section of pine-studded hills and a share of the Laramie Plains to graze. A bigger share, now that Ike Lafferty's outfit was wiped out.

But it all seemed worthless. He trudged out of the ashes, then stopped. He didn't even know where to stand, what to do, how to start. He joined the horse and the two sacred bulls under the little pine. Casino's reins made a circle on the ground where they dangled from his bridle. Good horse. Never stepped on a rein. He wished he had a dozen like him. Needed them, too, now that the Lafferty boys had run off all his other mounts.

As he sat down under the tree, he pulled his whiskey flask from a pocket, not bothering to check his watch. He took a big swallow and leaned back, letting the tree trunk push his hat over his eyes. For the past couple of weeks, since leaving her without a goodbye in the mountains, he had thought of almost nothing but Correen.

"You've got it bad this time, boy," Dusty was saying to him. He could conjure his partner's face now. Clearly, as if they had parted only yesterday. Dusty would be eleven years older, wouldn't he? Wouldn't there be a few more lines on the face? It didn't matter. Flesh aged, not the soul.

It wasn't Dusty he wanted to see, anyway, but Correen. He wondered where she was. Rebuilding her place in the foothills? If so, Lone Wolf was there with her. Or maybe she had gone with him back to Texas. He would have to find out when the rewards came, to send them their shares. He was hoping they had gone back to Texas. Didn't want to see them together. He wanted to see Correen, of course, but he didn't care to look at Lone Wolf again as long as he lived.

Now that it was all over, he was having nightmares about Wolverton. In the worst one, he and Lone Wolf were friends, standing the rigid corpse of the squaw up against a tree, giving it a haircut to resemble Lone Wolf's, then scalping it. It had really happened, of course, but in the dream they enjoyed it—laughing like ghouls as they worked. Then the corpse would come to life and start screaming, and Claude would wake in a cold sweat, his heart beating so hard that it hurt.

So he hadn't slept nights much lately, and now the sun was warming him, making him drowsy. He heard her voice: "Aren't you going to say goodbye?" But then he saw her embracing Wolverton. She had touched him a few times, too, to straighten his sideburns or bandage his injured hand. But there hadn't been any hugging between them.

Better to doze. Forget about her for a while. He scratched his beard, three weeks old now and still itching. It was going to have to come off.

* * *

The squeak and rattle of a rolling wagon woke him, and he jumped up from the ground, knocking his hat aside, dropping his whiskey flask, feeling for his pistols. Casino bolted, startled. The big paint stepped on a rein, broke it off.

Damn, nothing was certain anymore, he thought, trying to make his eyes focus on the road. He found the wagon, two mules, a cargo of odds and ends—and Correen with the reins in her hands, perched lightly on the seat like mist in the air, her hair tied back and bouncing on the wind behind her pretty face.

He rubbed his eyes and took a few steps toward her. Should he wave? What did she want?

He pulled himself together, picked up his hat, raked back his long hair, and fixed the felt crown over it. He waited until she stopped the team, then approached her, his heart gushing blood in his chest.

"What brings you here?" he said carefully.

She set the brake, wrapped the reins around the handle. She looked at him and shrugged. "I came for my reward." She sprang down from the wagon, landing flat-footed beside the front wheel.

"It ain't come yet."

"Perhaps I'll wait for it." She looked around at the ashes, wondering what his place had looked like before the Lafferty boys raided. "A wee bonnie croft you have here, Mr. Duval," she said, laying the lilt on thick.

Claude's eyes shifted, and his tongue felt his front teeth. "Where's Lone Wolf?"

She started walking slowly toward him, like a lioness stalking something. "He went back to Texas, of course."

He studied the stuff in the wagon, knowing she was reading his eyes. What was this, anyway? "You goin' after him?"

She stopped in her tracks. "Why would I?" She looked at him suspiciously.

Claude guarded himself, circled away from her, toward the wagon team. He had to remind himself of what he had seen up there. She had made him feel like a helpless fool. Not again . . . "He ran out on you, did he?"

She put her small hands on the curve of her hips. "Whatever do you mean?"

He nodded knowingly, circling the sun to his back, judging the cargo in the wagon. "So now you come crawlin' to your second choice?" He saw the astonishment in her face turn to anger and knew he had picked a bad fight.

"You bloody fool," she growled. "Surely you don't think . . ."

Did he think? He groped desperately for ammunition. "I had my eye on you two up there. Every time I'd come back to camp, there you'd be." He pointed his finger at her as if something had just occurred to him. "And I saw the way you hugged on him that last mornin'."

She gasped. "He had just saved my life!"

"I had a little to do with it, too, but you didn't hug me that way."

She took two menacing steps toward him. "It would have meant something entirely different with you, and it wasn't the time nor the place to start skylarkin' up there."

"And what about you standin' in my way to protect him," he went on, only now interpreting what she had last said.

"Didn't I do so for your sake, not his? If you

had murdered him, you would have lived the rest of your life as he must, and you would be of no use to me whatsoever."

Claude glared for a moment, then stomped his foot like a five-year-old. "You didn't have to go huggin' him!"

She laughed, flailing her arms. "I don't believe it. You're jealous of him. You are actually jealous of a single hug."

"Jealous?" He scoffed. "I am not!"

"You are! Do you think I ever felt the least bit attracted to him?" He turned away from her, but she circled and got in front of him. "That big, awkward ox of a man? His eyes squint like old bullet wounds in his head. Not like those poor, tortured, blind eyes of yours." She grabbed his arm and pressed her small fingers against his palm. "His hands are petrified, compared to these. These are warm and strong. He's an old killer, Mr. Duval. I could never condone the things he's done." She glared a warning at him. "I'm not that forgivin'."

Claude moved his mouth in an attempt to speak, but nothing came out. He wrapped his hand around hers, closing it gently.

Her eyes softened, and she shook her head in wonder. "You poor jealous fool. Can't you see what you've done? You did more than save my life. You rescued me." She leaned into him, put an arm around the back of his neck, and lifted herself toward his lips.

Claude felt himself weakening in her powerful embrace, drew back only an inch as her face neared his. "I thought you said you came here for your reward." He felt her hand slip from his and touch the small of his back, her fingers curling in against him like the claws of a playful cat.

"Perhaps I came to deliver one as well."

Claude slipped his arms around her and pressed his lips down on hers. For two weeks—delivering Giff Dearborn, herding the bremmers down from the mountains—he had sulked and thought of this. He had lain on his back alone at night to watch Dusty's star pass over him. Maybe Lone Wolf was right. Maybe there were no accidents. Maybe the humpbacked cattle really were sacred, the mountains possessed of real medicine. Maybe even the Creedmoor had been wrought by God's hand.

She pushed away from him, her cheeks reddened where his beard had scratched her. She ran her fingers roughly through his whiskers.

"Mr. Duval," she said, shaking her head, "you're badly needin' a shave."

Printed in the USA
CPSIA information can be obtained
at www.ICGtesting.com
LVHW091815130624
783112LV00003B/337